Secret Death

Detective Inspector Paul Amos Mystery series Book 6

RODNEY HOBSON

First published 2018 by Sharpe Books.

ISBN: 9781791734022

CONTENTS

Secret Death
Detective Inspector Paul Amos Mystery Series Book 6

CHAPTER 1

It was a beautiful morning in May in the 1990s and Detective Inspector Paul Amos drew the short straw. It was his own fault and it led him, and his detective sergeant Juliet Swift, into the most frustrating case he encountered in his career with the Lincolnshire Police Force.

As he entered police headquarters, a woman aged about 55 was in full, if slightly incoherent, flood with Mark Jenkins, the desk sergeant, the reluctant recipient of her tidings. Jenkins had, as Amos well knew, often remarked that the whole point of moving HQ from the centre of Lincoln to a new building in Nettleham three miles east of the county town was to discourage members of the public from walking in and reporting crimes.

"I've come all the way from Alford to tell you about this," the woman was saying. "I didn't know whether I should – my husband told me not to but my friend Jane said I ought to, it's my civic duty," she said.

"Do you know how difficult it is to get here from Alford these days?"

Amos could see from Jenkins' face that he wished it was more difficult. The woman took the lack of a verbal response to indicate that the desk sergeant wanted her to tell him.

"I could have waited until tomorrow and driven here," she said. "My husband Bob needed the car today. Jane said if I kept putting it off I'd never do it.

"I had to get the bus to Louth," she continued, "then the Lincoln bus from Louth. It should have come straight through but we had to change at Horncastle onto the one from Skegness, which is always a pain because you wonder if the driver will try to make you buy another ticket, I much prefer it

1

when they come straight through, well it does save so much messing but you don't always have the choice.

"I would have given up and turned back at Horncastle but I remembered that Jane had said it was my duty ..."

Sgt Jenkins had been attempting to sort out some paperwork surreptitiously under the counter but it was hard for him to concentrate in the face of the breathless barrage. He looked up.

"What exactly is it you have come to report?" he asked, his customary patient courtesy tainted a little with exasperation.

"I'm not exactly sure," the woman replied, having taken the opportunity of refilling her lungs with fresh breath. "That's the problem. I'm not entirely sure that there is anything to report. But I do think I should talk to a detective. And it was a long walk from the nearest bus stop even when I got here, not that I'm blaming you personally, of course."

Jenkins sighed, looked at the woman then caught sight of Amos hovering just inside the doorway.

The inspector had delayed too long. He felt some obligation to relieve Jenkins of his burden. After all, the sergeant had provided vital information in his latest, recently concluded, big case. There was now an unusual lull in CID. Biting the bullet, Amos stepped forward decisively.

"Detective Inspector Paul Amos at your service, madam," he announced pompously to Jenkins' relief and amusement. "Why don't you come through to CID and tell me all about it?"

Amos ushered the woman through to his private office, which he hardly used because he hated to be separated from his staff. He had a feeling that this particular interview would be painfully fruitless, so it was better to keep it from the rest of the department.

The woman accepted the offer of a seat but declined tea or coffee, despite repeating how long it had been since she had resolved over breakfast to do her duty. Amos was desperate for a caffeine-laden coffee but could hardly get one just for himself.

"Can we start with your name, please?" Amos said firmly before the woman could launch off at another tangent.

"Elizabeth Wareham."

"And you live at Alford, I gather," Amos again cut in to keep the woman to basics.

Amos knew the market town of Alford, to the southeast of Louth and halfway to the coast, from his time in Skegness as a young police officer. He had rarely ventured that way since moving to HQ in Lincoln, though.

Holidaymakers from the Midlands would wind through it en route to Mablethorpe or Sutton-on-Sea. Apart from the annual Easter clog dancing festival in the market place just to the south of the main road, the town had always seemed unremarkable to him.

"Yes, on Willoughby Road," the woman was saying. "That's the road that runs from the market place towards Willoughby. That's why it's called Willoughby Road," Wareham explained unnecessarily.

"Yes, quite," Amos said out loud. Silently, he added: "This is going to be like pulling teeth. What on earth possessed me to rescue Mark from this woman."

Instead, he actually said: "And what precisely is troubling you?"

The accent was on the word precisely.

"It's my friend Stella. Well, she's not really my friend, just a neighbour. She doesn't say much."

That's a relief, Amos thought. In the unlikely event that this comes to anything, a little reticence might prove a blessing.

"What did she do, your friend, I mean neighbour, Stella?"

"It wasn't her," came the emphatic reply. "It was her brother. He died."

"Go on," Amos said, sitting up sharply, his curiosity aroused.

"Not that anyone would have known," Elizabeth Wareham continued with a distinct hint of indignation. "If I hadn't happened to see the ambulance outside the house the night he was taken ill I'd probably never have found out to this day."

"But presumably Stella would have told you the next time she saw you if you hadn't seen the ambulance for yourself," Amos protested.

"That's the point," came the forceful reply. "When I saw her the next day and asked how her brother was she refused to talk about it. She wouldn't say what was wrong with him or which hospital he'd been taken to. I had to ring round the hospitals pretending to be a relative until Lincoln County Hospital admitted to having him, and even then all they would say was that he was as well as could be expected.

"That was no use. I didn't know what to expect because I didn't know what he had been admitted for. I rang in the evening and they said he had passed away peacefully."

"So he died under medical care," Amos said, his interest rapidly waning. "I don't see why you think this might be a police matter."

"I haven't finished the story yet," Wareham said impatiently as if rebuking a tiresome schoolboy. "Stella still wouldn't say why her brother had been rushed to hospital or what he had died of. In fact, she wouldn't even admit he had died.

"I know he'd had heart trouble and he'd been a bit poorly now and then – vomiting, stomach cramps, diarrhoea. It was ever since he and Stella came back from that cruise to see the Northern lights, well you're with all these strange people, it's asking for trouble."

"She wouldn't admit he died," Amos reminder her.

"At first I thought it was the shock of her brother passing away so suddenly. Well, we all grieve in our own way, don't we? Not that she was particularly close to her brother. I took her round a casserole just to make sure she was eating properly and she was downright rude. She refused to accept it point blank on the doorstep and she wouldn't even let me in the house. I was really put out, I can tell you."

"Come back to your story, Mrs Wareham," Amos said gently but persuasively. He assumed she was a Mrs from the gold band and engagement ring on her left ring finger.

The woman before him looked doubtful about being told what to do but she had, after all, secured the attention of a detective inspector, no less.

"I kept asking her when the funeral was going to be – and so did other people. I could understand her not telling Phyllis

Jones. She goes to all the funerals just so she can get a free tea. Well, naturally we wanted to pay our respects. Not that any of us particularly liked Oscar – that was his name, although everyone called him Ossie for short. He ran a second hand junk shop in Alford, though I don't see how he could have made any money out of it."

"And what did she say about the funeral?" Amos diverted her back to the main narrative.

"Nothing. Just like his mystery illness in the first place. She wouldn't tell anyone when or where the funeral would be. Not even who the funeral directors were. There's only two in the town so I rang them both but neither of them would confirm they were handling the arrangements.

"But next day I saw one of them call at Stella's house so I knew they were doing it. Guess what they said when I rang them again and told them I'd seen them so I knew they were handling the funeral."

"Please just tell me," Amos said.

"They said they were under strict instructions not to discuss the matter with anyone. I was completely dumfounded. Well, I protested, of course, but I wish I'd saved my breath. They wouldn't budge."

"So I take it you missed the funeral?"

"Ah, that's where you're wrong," Wareham said triumphantly. "I happened to be in the centre of Alford when I spotted Stella getting into a car behind a hearse with a coffin in it. She was the only one in the car apart from the driver.

"I dashed back home and got in my car. Bob – my husband – taught me to drive and although I was very nervous I took the test in Skegness where it's easier to pass because there are no hills and not much traffic out of the holiday season."

"You got in the car and ..." Amos persisted.

"I drove up the road to follow them. I don't normally drive fast, especially in Alford because people know me, but I didn't want to lose them."

"And did you? Lose them, that is."

"Well, it was a bit stupid to think I could run all the way home and drive back again before they'd set off. There was no sign of them at the church. I didn't think there would be. It wouldn't have been worth getting in a car for that short distance from the funeral director's.

"So I tried to catch them up before they got to Ulceby Cross because I didn't know if they would be going to Boston or Grimsby crematorium, they're both the same distance, it's such a long way to go."

"And did you? Did you catch them?"

"No. It was very annoying. They don't half crack on once they're out of town. It's very disrespectful and I daren't drive all that fast. Anyway, I had to take a guess. I thought Boston. Well, Stella couldn't abide Grimsby. It's so run down now, she always complains, since they lost all the trawlers."

"Boston," Amos interrupted again. "Were you right?"

"As it happens, yes. There they were, waiting for their turn. The previous funeral had overrun so they had to wait. Well, it's like a production line at the crem. Not like a proper church burial.

"They were just moving up when I arrived so I parked in the visitors' car park and got to the door just as Stella was following the coffin in. She turned round and barred my way. She absolutely forbade me from entering. Naturally I demanded to know why she was not allowing anyone to attend her brother's funeral.

"And that's when she said it."

"Said what, Mrs Wareham?"

"She said: 'Because I don't know which one of you murdered him'."

Chapter 2

Having delivered her punchline and having thus fulfilled the obligations of duty in accordance with her conscience, Elizabeth Wareham was all for leaving it at that. She rose to her feet and made as if to depart.

Amos had been taken aback by the bluntness of her final sentence after so much waffle.

"Please sit down, Mrs Wareham," he said quickly. "I'd better write down a few details."

"So you think it's true – that he really was murdered?" Wareham said in a shocked tone as she resumed her seat.

"I don't know," Amos replied truthfully. "But now you've made a report I'm obliged to take it seriously."

He extracted the address of Stella Dover and the name of the relevant funeral director. Elizabeth Wareham could not think of anyone who would want Oscar Dover dead nor any possible motive.

She declined the offer of a lift home in a police car, saying she would walk back to the A153 and wait for the next bus.

Amos was still staring at the sheet of paper on his desk when Detective Sergeant Juliet Swift tapped lightly on the window between Amos's office and the CID department. Amos waved her in.

"Who on earth was that?" Swift asked. "I took it you didn't want to be disturbed."

"I'm thankful for small mercies," Amos said. "She digressed quite enough without the extra benefit on an interruption."

He gave Swift a resumé of the relevant parts of Elizabeth Wareham's report.

"Did you take her seriously?" Swift asked. It was a genuine question.

"I really don't know," Amos replied. "Everything tells me not to. Yet I don't believe Mrs Wareham would make up the bit about the murder accusation. She took too much trouble to get here.

"The obvious problem is the fact that Oscar Dover's body was cremated, so there's no way of turning something up in a post mortem. It will be pretty much impossible to prove it even if he was in fact murdered."

"Do you think that Elizabeth Wareham could have killed him?" Swift asked suddenly. "She sounds a bit of a nutter. She could be taunting us, knowing we can't possibly prove she did it. You know as well as I do we get weirdos admitting to crimes they didn't commit. It's only one step further to report a crime you actually have done, just for the hell of it, not expecting to be taken seriously."

Amos thought for a few moments.

"It's possible," he admitted eventually, "but I don't think she has the wit or the deviousness for that. However, if you're right that pushes me even further towards my initial inclination not to investigate the case. I wouldn't want to give her the pleasure of seeing us waste our time on a wild goose chase."

"Well, here's something that may change your mind," Swift said with a wry smile. "I hear a rumour that the Chief Constable is looking for a volunteer to help him for a few weeks with his latest project. It may be advantageous to be out of HQ today."

Amos sat up with a start. The Chief Constable was notorious for launching a new campaign at irregular intervals and pursuing it with vigour before losing interest rapidly. There then followed an uneasy period of inactivity before he got the next bee in his bonnet.

"What is it?" he asked anxiously.

"I don't know," Swift replied, "but you get sucked in at your peril. Besides, I've never visited Alford. There's nothing very exciting to keep us here at the moment. It'll make a nice day out."

Amos knew she was right. A few minutes later they were driving at a leisurely speed along the A153 towards Horncastle before meandering through small villages dotting the Lincolnshire Wolds as they took the scenic route to the large roundabout at Ulceby Cross, where Amos selected the road sloping down gently into Alford.

"I propose to try the undertaker first," he said as they entered the town. "Unless he's poisoning people to drum up trade he should be a totally impartial bystander.

"At least we should be able to accomplish that before Elizabeth Wareham has time to get back and see us making fools of ourselves. The other advantage of trying him first is that is that if he's out at a funeral we can always come back to him later."

As soon as she learnt the reason for the officers' visit, the young woman on reception quickly ushered them through to a private room where she introduced them to an elderly, greying man called Frank Dickinson who displayed all the gloomy air of quiet, insincere reassurance so beloved in funeral directors.

"These police officers have come about Mr Oscar Dover," she announced peremptorily.

"Oh," Dickinson said sharply as his assistant beat a hasty retreat. Slightly reluctantly, he invited Amos and Swift to sit down.

"It's just a routine inquiry," Amos said in a conciliatory tone. "We just want to ask you about a man called Oscar Dover, as your assistant indicated. I believe you handled the arrangements."

"I'm afraid I really can't discuss the matter, officer," Dickinson replied with irritating smoothness. "Client confidentiality."

"Client confidentiality!" Swift gasped. "Your clients are all dead!"

"Not so," the lugubrious funeral director responded. "Of course, if you are of a religious disposition you no doubt regard a funeral as smoothing the passage of the departed soul to a better place. We respect that view, naturally. Our role, however, is to comfort those left behind.

"Our clients are the living. Specifically, if you'll forgive my saying so, whoever requests, and pays for, our services."

Amos was in a quandary. Normally he would demand cooperation in a murder inquiry, which in his view took precedence over all other considerations. However, he did not fully accept that any crime had actually taken place and he did not wish to make a big issue of the inquiry at this stage.

"I understand in this case your client was Stella Dover, the deceased's sister," he said.

"I can only confirm that if Miss Dover gives us permission to do so," Dickinson replied, thus inadvertently confirming that she was indeed the client.

"Did you put a notice about the funeral in the local edition of the Lincolnshire Standard? We can check with the paper so you wouldn't be giving anything away."

"No such notice was placed by us."

"Isn't that rather unusual?"

"It is, but every funeral is different. We are quite meticulous in carrying out the client's wishes. Not that I am confirming that this is what happened in this case," Dickinson added hastily, "or even that Miss Dover was our client."

"The funeral was at Boston Crematorium, I believe," Amos said. "Again we can check but it will take longer."

"I believe it was."

"Who officiated?"

"Now you're asking me for specific details, officer, though I can point out that no clergy are required at a cremation, or indeed any funeral."

Amos rose to his feet and Swift promptly did likewise.

"Thank you for your time, Mr Dickinson," the inspector said. "I must ask you to use as much discretion in not mentioning our visit to anyone as you have done in protecting your client."

Dickinson also stood up.

"Of course," he said reassuringly.

Chapter 3

"Is it worth going on?" Amos said wearily as he and Swift returned to the car.

"I must admit I didn't honestly think it was worth turning out in the first place," Swift replied, "but now I'm quite intrigued. I've inevitably talked to funeral directors in the course of this job, and you must have talked to more than me. Have you ever heard one quote client confidentiality at you?"

Amos shook his head.

"There clearly is something very odd about this," Swift went on. "I vote we try this Stella Dover woman and see if it leads anywhere."

"You're right, of course," Amos said. "We might as well see this through. If we spin it out we can have afternoon tea at the windmill on the Mablethorpe road."

The main road took a semi-circular route round the bulge of the parish church but Amos swung down past the market place and into the narrow road towards Willoughby. Almost immediately they reached the address that Elizabeth Wareham had supplied for Stella Dover.

Wareham had given the house number. What she hadn't mentioned was the house name: Lyngbakr's Lair.

It adorned a large enamel nameplate next to the front door, the curious name superimposed on the image of a fisherman and the outline of an island.

Swift gasped.

"Have you ever seen a house name like that? Whatever happened to Dunromin? Is that supposed to be the Isle of Wight?"

Amos simply raised his eyebrows. He had already rung the doorbell and before he could reply an elderly woman opened the door. She was apparently of sharp hearing.

"It was there when I moved in," she said tartly to Swift.

The reception that the officers received when Amos

introduced himself and Swift was not what they were expecting.

"I suppose you've come about the court case," the woman said. "You'd better come in. I didn't think you were taking it seriously."

Amos entered quickly while he had the opportunity, neither confirming nor denying that the visit concerned any court case, not least because he had no idea what the woman was referring to.

"I take it you are Stella Dover," he said once they were all seated. "Tell me about the court case."

"Hmmph!" came the reply. "Yes, I'm Stella Dover. I told the officer at Alford police station all about it. Don't tell me he hasn't passed the information on. I might have known it. He wasn't paying proper attention."

"It's much better if I get it from you first hand," Amos replied reassuringly. "Especially if, as you say, the officer you spoke to didn't take proper notice."

"It's Oscar's eldest daughter," came the response. "She's barred me from my own home. I told Oscar to make a proper will. She can't shut me out of my own home, can she? I'm as much entitled to it as she is. Why should I have to take her to court just to get into my own home?"

"I don't quite understand, Miss Dover," Amos said, perplexed. "Isn't this your home?"

The question provoked another "Hmmph" conveying a blend of irritation and disgust.

"I knew that constable wasn't taking proper notice," Dover said. "I should have insisted on seeing a superior officer."

"You've got one now, Miss Dover," Amos said gently. "Make the most of it. We've come all the way from Lincoln."

This mollified her considerably.

"Oh well," she sighed, "I'll go through the whole story again.

"Oscar's wife died very young, leaving him with two young daughters to bring up. They were living at the time in our family home – the one that had belonged to our parents."

"Had your parents died by then?"

12

"Dad had died and Mum was in a nursing home so it made sense for Oscar and his family to move in to our parents' house, always on the understanding, of course, that I retained a half share in the house when Mum died.

"Poor Oscar was utterly devastated. He faced losing his job as well as his wife. Luckily he had me to rescue the situation. Not that I got much thanks for it. I moved in and ran the household and told him to pull himself together."

"That must have been quite a sacrifice on your part," Amos said sympathetically. "Did you have to give up your own home?"

"I was living here in this house," Stella Dover said, "and had a good job, too. Luckily I was able to rent it to a young couple who couldn't afford to buy. Five years later Oscar remarried, more fool him, and I moved back here as soon as I could."

"Yes, it's difficult with second marriages," Amos said. "It must have been hard for the girls. They would still be quite young and missing their mother. It would have been difficult for them to cope with."

"Hmmph," Dover said. "I daresay, but it was their own stupid fault, particularly the eldest. I put a bit of discipline into their lives. Well, they needed it. Jill – that's Oscar's first wife – let them do as they pleased.

"I had a real time of it, getting them to wash the back of their necks, pick their clothes up instead of leaving them lying on the floor, sitting properly at the table for their meals. They didn't know what was good for them.

"They soon found out. When Oscar remarried, it was out of the frying pan and into the fire. I came back here, of course. I wasn't going to stay there while that woman was in the house."

"I understand your brother was living here with you when he died recently," Amos said. "Had he parted from his second wife?"

"It lasted about three or four years until she went off with another old fool. She'd pretty much bled poor Oscar dry by then. He'd worked himself to the bone slaving over her. There wasn't much apart from the house and the furniture left.

"Oscar was completely broken by it all. At least by then the girls were old enough to fend for themselves. So guess who had to step up to the mark again? Yours truly."

Stella Dover was now well into her stride, fuelled by righteous indignation.

"So you moved back once again?" Amos asked.

"No, absolutely not," came the emphatic reply. "I wasn't going through all that again. The girls were completely out of control. I wasn't going to be treated with sullen ingratitude for a second time. No, I told Oscar he had to move in with me."

"So that's how he came to be here living with you when he died," Amos said. "What happened to the girls?"

"Hmmph. That's the whole point. Nothing happened to the girls. The girls got the house. That's what I'm complaining about. It's theft, pure and simple."

"The girls are still living in your brother Oscar's house?"

"Not Oscar's house. <u>Our</u> house. The family house. It was meant to be divided between me and Oscar."

"How come, then, he and his family have lived there all these years and you have had a house here?"

"Hmmph. Oscar was the executor of our parent's wills. And he had power of attorney for our mother. He had control of it all. There was nothing I could do. I told him often enough but there it is," Dover said turning to DS Swift, "men never take any notice, do they?"

Swift nodded, hoping the gesture looked sympathetic rather than sardonic.

"I finally got Oscar to talk to his elder daughter, Julia," Dover continued. "She's a little minx. I wanted to go with him but she refused to see him unless he went alone. They must have had a blazing row because he came back very subdued.

"And do you know what the little devil told him?"

Here Stella Dover paused for effect.

"That I was barred from setting foot in <u>her</u> – her, mark you – house ever again."

"Presumably you had the opportunity to talk to her about it at your brother's funeral?" Amos asked innocently.

This produced the most emphatic "Hmmph" of all.

"She didn't come to the funeral. Neither her nor her sister. Fancy missing your own father's funeral. Guilty conscience if you ask me. I think she killed him."

Amos sat up sharply.

"You think she killed him?" he asked incredulously.

Stella Dover paused for a few moments and the suspicion of a supressed smile played around her lips.

"I'm suggesting she broke his heart with her callous behaviour," she finally said. "He died a broken man. And it was all her fault."

Chapter 4

Amos sat back and thought for several seconds, to Stella Dover's evident satisfaction.

"You'd better give us the address of the family home and the names and ages of your two nieces," he said eventually.

Dover provided the requested information.

As the officers left, her parting shot was: "All I want is my home back. I only want what is rightfully mine."

The officers drove to the market square and parked in order to swap thoughts. Amos hated to let anyone who had been interviewed see that they were talking over the information.

"Well," he said, "we always knew this was likely to be a waste of time. This is obviously a matter between Stella Dover and her nieces. It's not a criminal issue at all."

To the inspector's surprise, his detective sergeant took a different view.

"I must admit," she said, "that my curiosity has been aroused. She complains that her nieces didn't come to the funeral yet made no mention of keeping the details secret – assuming that woman who spoke to you at headquarters was telling the truth. Nor of accusing all and sundry of killing her brother."

"I have no doubt that Elizabeth Wareham, the woman who reported the incident, was telling the truth," Amos admitted. "She was clearly deeply troubled by the whole matter. So yes, it is curious that Stella Dover passed up the opportunity to make the same accusation to two detectives."

"I think she is a highly manipulative woman," Swift said. "I must say I'd like to know what her nieces think about it all."

"It's getting towards lunchtime," Amos said. "The young ladies live in Louth. There's a decent chippie there."

"I feel like we're playing truant," Swift said, "but I do fancy fish and chips. I skipped breakfast and I'm starving."

"We'll have to pay for it ourselves," Amos said. "I really

can't justify claiming this on expenses when, like you, I feel like we're playing truant.

"And by the way, this is your inquiry from now on. You can talk to the girls. The only thing I would suggest is that you don't call it a murder inquiry."

An early lunch had the merit of bringing Amos and Swift to the nieces' house at 1pm, when there was a fair chance of someone being at home for a midday meal. In the event, Julia, the elder girl, was at work according to her younger sister, Lynn, who opened the door to the two detectives.

Lynn explained that she was taking A levels and on days when there was no examination, pupils were allowed to study at home.

Amos had to pick up a school blazer tossed nonchalantly on a chair in order to sit down. He placed it carefully on the chair arm with the badge, incorporating the school's name, clearly showing as a reminder of what was supposed to be occupying her mind.

The absence of any schoolbooks and the presence of several celebrity-watching magazines suggested that the concept of home study was having limited success.

One magazine lay open on the chair that Swift selected. As she made to close it, Lynn leapt forward and grabbed it to avoid losing the page.

"We've been talking to your aunt," Swift tried as an opening gambit. She hated not coming straight to the point. "We understand there is some problem regarding this house."

"No there isn't," Lynn said abruptly. "We own it and we live in it. Julia and me. End of story."

"Can we go back to the start of the story," Swift said firmly. "As I understand it, the house was left by your paternal grandparents to both your father and your aunt."

"Hmmph," Lynn said in an odd echo of her aunt. "It never belonged to Aunt Stella. Dad put the house in our names, mine and Julia's. We own it. We always have. She has her own house."

"But your aunt moved in for a time, though."

"Only because Dad couldn't cope when Mum died. And a

real pain she was, too. She soon cleared off when Dad remarried."

"You've had a lot of upheaval in your life," Swift said with fake sympathy. This did not bring the response she hoped for.

"Look, what is this?" Lynn demanded. "A session on the bloody psychiatrist's couch? I don't see what this has got to do with the police. We're not growing cannabis."

Once again the opportunity to drop the case stared the police officers in the face. Once again, fate contrived to draw them back in.

Julia returned home unexpectedly.

The elder of the two nieces of Stella Dover entered the house in a distinctly foul mood. She was particularly unamused to find two police officers in her front room.

"Bloody Job Centre," she said vehemently before her language deteriorated markedly. "I suppose they've sent you to check up on me," she interjected between expletives. "Bloody Job Centre. I'm only earning what I'm allowed."

"We're not from the Job Centre so you can tone down the obscenities," Swift said sternly. "Your aunt has made a complaint."

"Oh, do let me guess," Julia said sarcastically. "No need to ask which one. Bloody Aunt Stella."

"You have more than one aunt?"

"Never mind how many bloody aunties we've got. What's she been saying?"

"That you are barring her from entering her own house, or at least one that she has a half share in."

"That's a police matter, is it?" Julia said defiantly. "This is our house in our name. Nan and Grandad always intended us to have it. Aunt Stella wanted to build a granny flat at the back so she could move in. Well, we weren't having her back, the manipulative little bitch. She's welcome to visit, not to stay."

"Is that what you had a blazing row with your Dad about just before he died?" Swift asked.

Amos shifted in his seat. The questioning was getting nowhere. He was seriously regretting ever embarking on this pointless excursion.

The latest question did, however, enliven proceedings by producing another round of obscenities. Eventually Julia answered.

"No I didn't," she said indignantly. "I just put him straight about the way Auntie Stella was manipulating him. She'd put him up to asking us to let her move back in here. No bloody way, I told him.

"It was the stress she caused him that killed him," she added bitterly.

"Did your aunt raise the matter with you at your father's funeral," Swift asked innocently.

Another round of unsavoury language emerged from Julia's lips. For the first time her face showed an emotion other than defiance. She was close to tears.

"We weren't at Dad's funeral," she said in anguish. "We didn't know anything about it. We didn't know he had died. We didn't even know he had been rushed to hospital.

"He never wanted to be cremated. He told everyone he wanted to be buried with Mum."

Chapter 5

It was mid-afternoon when Amos and Swift arrived back at HQ.

They said nothing on the way back. There was nothing to say. They had both known the inquiry was almost certainly going to hit a dead end so there were no recriminations.

As he entered CID, Amos had an uneasy feeling that was augmented by the slightly amused expression on Jennifer's beautiful young smiling face.

Amos felt disconcerted. Jennifer had been imposed on him by the Chief Constable, Sir Robert Fletcher, as an administrative assistant. Despite Amos's early reservations, they had built a bond until, recently, Amos had begun to suspect that she was spying on him.

Had she reported to the Chief Constable that he and Swift had been playing truant for most of the day?

"I've cleared up all the admin from your last case," Jennifer said sweetly. "The papers that need signing are laid out on your desk."

Amos relaxed for a moment, leaving him open to the sucker punch.

"And Sir Robert is very keen to talk to you in his office."

Amos responded with only a cursory nod and went straight to the Chief Constable's domain on the top floor, using the lift so as not to arrive breathless. He was ushered in by Sir Robert's highly nervous personal assistant David, but without David's customary glare of disapproval.

"Ah, Paul, come in, come in," Sir Robert Fletcher called out enthusiastically to Amos's surprise.

First names were usually reserved for those in favour with the Chief Constable, and Amos had no cause to believe that this accolade applied to him at this particular moment. It rarely did.

"Have a seat, Paul," Sir Robert continued warmly. "This is

right up your street."

Amos sank into the chair on the opposite side of the desk to the Chief Constable and his heart sank in similar fashion.

"I have an exciting project about to be launched and it needs your expert guiding hand. I want police officers to visit every school in the county. David here is drawing up a list so you needn't worry about the administrative details, which I know you hate. I gather you've nothing important on at the moment."

No Chief Constable, least of all Sir Robert, could be expected to know the minutiae of what was happening in CID. Had Jennifer done the dirty on him, Amos wondered. However, he had better pay attention to Sir Robert now and worry about Jennifer later.

"I'll need you to co-ordinate officers in all areas. David will help with the arrangements," Fletcher continued. He was staring out of the window, probably imagining a vista of schools with police officers entering their portals purposefully.

The look of dismay on David's face at the thought of having to work with Amos was the only element of relief in a potentially dire situation.

"We'll need uniformed officers and detectives on a scheme this big."

Sir Robert was getting into his stride.

"The best way to tackle crime is to deflect young people from breaking the law in the first place," he said. "If you do well, this could be a permanent role for you."

Amos heartily agreed with the sentiment. He just didn't want to be the instrument by which the policy was implemented. He had entered the police force first and foremost to solve crimes, not prevent them.

"We have a potential murder inquiry," Amos protested feebly. "A report of a suspicious death."

"Your sergeant can deal with it," Fletcher said curtly, swinging round from the window and looking Amos squarely in the face.

"What's she called? Speed?"

"Swift," Amos corrected.

"Yes, yes, Julia Swift."

Amos decided another correction would be undiplomatic. Julia Swift was near enough.

"We're a modern police force and we must give young women like Julia a chance."

It was news to Amos that the Chief Constable was such a feminist. Sir Robert was by no means a misogynist but he did always, by default rather than intent, favour male rather than female officers as part of the natural order of things.

Amos was glad to give Swift a chance. She deserved it and would make the most of the opportunity. He just wished it wasn't at the expense of him having to take on the thankless task of working on the Chief Constable's new pet project, especially if he was to play a leading role.

"Should she be made up to acting inspector, perhaps?" Amos asked tentatively. His motive was not entirely altruistic. It would mean paying Swift more until he returned to CID and extra costs would probably hasten the end of the project.

The Chief Constable showed no signs of hearing the question.

"You've got good contacts in the press, Paul," Sir Robert was saying, oblivious to the many times that he had castigated Amos for leaking stories instead of going through official press releases. "Now's your chance to put that to good use. We launch Operation Education tomorrow."

"There's good and bad news," Amos told Swift on his crestfallen return to CID. "The bad news is that I'm hors de combat until the Chief Constable gets over his latest obsession."

He explained to his sergeant the bare bones of his new and, he hoped, temporary role. He took no comfort from having learnt in the course of his working life that it was the permanent roles that never seemed to last while the temporary roles usually went on for ever.

"You'd better tell me the good news," Swift asked wryly.

"You're in charge of the team in the meantime."

Swift snorted.

"Do I get to be acting detective inspector? Do I get more

money?" She asked.

Amos shook his head in response to both questions.

"I did ask," he answered truthfully, "but I'm afraid Sir Robert is thinking about nothing else other than the project, as he always does when he gets a bee in his bonnet."

The conversation was conducted, deliberately on Amos's part, next to Jennifer's desk so she could hear every word. If she reported it all back to the Chief Constable and Amos was taken off the education project in disgrace, that was better than being trapped in it.

However, when Amos arrived at Lincolnshire Police Headquarters the following morning, he was waylaid by David and ushered up to a newly refurbished office on the top floor, next to David's office and just across the corridor from the Chief Constable.

Chapter 6

On a lower floor, Det Sgt Juliet Swift was making the most of her new-found freedom. There are those who crumble in the face of unexpected opportunity and those who rise to the occasion, she told herself. Amos showed no interest in early retirement. This opportunity might not come her way again aby time soon.

Crime was apparently still generally out of fashion in Lincoln. Swift despatched two constables in the team she had acquired from Amos to sort out a spate of minor burglaries down near Lincoln City football ground to the south of the county town, taking care to give Jennifer the impression that she was going with them.

Her contemptuous view of Jennifer was untarnished by the stunning beauty that so beguiled Amos. The two young women rarely spoke. Indeed, they barely acknowledged each other, though they were never less than civil.

Swift made her way to the carpark. There was little danger that she would be missed. If anything really interesting came up it would be allocated to a male colleague. Supposing, just supposing, she could make something of the mystery of Oscar Dover.

Once out of hearing of HQ, Swift switched on the siren and flashing lights of the unmarked police car and shot eastwards, sticking to main roads until she reached Ulceby Cross, then she switched off lights and siren on the last quiet stretch into Alford.

She noticed the Half Moon on her right as she entered the town. It was too early to try a pub for any gossip about the "murder victim" so Swift decided to tackle Stella Dover head on. She was greeted with the customary "Hmmph!"

"If you want anything done, send a woman," Dover said. "Typical man to duck out at the first opportunity and leave it to you. I could see he wasn't very interested."

"Miss Dover," Swift said. "We've talked to your nieces and unless you are prepared to make a formal complaint that they have committed fraud and make a statement to that effect, the question of your family home is a matter for a civil court to decide."

"Hmmph. I can't see why you bothered to come all this way to tell me that," Dover said peevishly.

"There is another reason," Swift said. "Miss Dover, do you have reason to believe that someone killed your brother?"

Stella Dover looked at Swift suspiciously.

"What have my nieces been telling you?" she demanded.

"Never mind who said what," Swift retorted sternly. "Please just answer the question."

"Not particularly."

"What do you mean, not particularly? Either you do or you don't."

Dover thought for several moments.

Then she said: "He died very quickly."

"A lot of people die quickly," Swift said dryly. She was trying not to let her desire to grasp control of her own murder case cloud her judgement.

"There was nothing wrong with him," Dover said. "Nothing at all."

Then, after a pause, she added: "Apart from his dickie heart."

"Is that what he died of?" Swift asked.

"Hmmph. That's what the hospital put on the death certificate. I don't think they knew. They just put that down because they didn't want the trouble of doing a post mortem. He was on medication. He hadn't had high blood pressure for years.

"I think he was poisoned. He was always getting sick. If they'd given him the proper tests at the hospital they could have saved him. I told the ambulance crew he'd been poisoned."

"But he lived here with you," Swift protested. "Didn't he have his meals here? Surely you're the only person who could have poisoned him."

"Hmmph. He was fine when I looked after him. He let himself go after Lucy left him. He used to sit in the café in the market place for hours on end. Anybody could have slipped something into his coffee."

"And do you think anyone had reason to?" Swift asked dubiously. "Did he have any enemies?"

"There were people who didn't like him," Dover said enigmatically. "He ran a junk shop, you know. He did house clearances. Paid a fee for the right to whatever was in there. Some people accused him of robbing them.

"OK, he made the occasional killing if he came across anything valuable. But most of the time it was hard work clearing out all the stuff and finding somewhere to store it. Nobody else wanted to do it. He always played fair but that didn't stop some people grumbling."

"Who grumbled?" Swift demanded. "Name names."

Dover leaned forward, almost thrusting her face into Swift's.

"I don't gossip and I don't make accusations," she said almost menacingly. "Let it drop."

Stella Dover was the one person who had suggested that her brother Oscar had been murdered. If she was reluctant to pursue the matter, then it was unlikely that any inquiry onto the circumstances of his death would get anywhere while Swift remained in Alford.

Reluctantly, she returned to police headquarters, picked up the phone and dialled Lincoln County Hospital. The switchboard answered promptly; getting through to administration took rather longer.

Some slow tune, unfamiliar to Swift, was played down the line as she waited. Was this meant to sound reassuring to anxious relatives or to soften them up for news that some loved one had passed away?

Swift memorised the tune. She would hum it back to Amos next time she saw him. He would know what it was. He seemed to know all the dirges.

Eventually a young, bored, female voice answered.

Swift identified herself and said: "I'm enquiring about a man called Oscar Dover."

"Uh huh."

Swift gave the date of admission, adding that the man in question had been taken in by ambulance and had died the following day.

"Died?" the dispassionate voice on the other end of the line repeated. "Died? He'll have been archived."

"So?"

"So the records'll be down in archives, not up here."

"Can you check whether they have been sent," Swift demanded. "I don't want to be put through to archives and find they are still with you."

"S'pose so," the voice said without enthusiasm. "Date of birth?"

"For heaven's sake," Swift said in exasperation. "How many Oscar Dovers have you admitted recently?"

"Date of birth?" the voice repeated dispassionately.

Was it a sign she was getting older, Swift wondered, that she found young people were getting more stupid? She must ask Amos about that, too.

This was a potential sticking point. Because there was no formal investigation, Swift had not had cause to take details of the man she was inquiring about. She searched through the papers on her desk just in case it was recorded somewhere.

Hallelujah! That busybody Elizabeth Wareham had actually stated Oscar Dover's date of birth among the details she had given to Amos. Swift supplied the required information to the voice at the other end of the line.

"Address?"

There was no point in further sarcasm. Swift gave the address as patiently as she could manage.

"Just putting you on hold while I check," the monotonous voice said. Before Swift could protest, another piece of music came on the line. This time the tune was brisk and cheerful, as if taunting her; this time the wait was longer than before.

Just as Swift was considering giving up, the music suddenly ceased and the voice returned.

"You're in luck," it said. "The records are still here. We're very busy, you know. We're getting further behind with the work. We need more staff. They should have gone down to archives by now."

"I need the names of the ambulance crew who brought him in and where they are based," Swift said without sympathy.

The ambulance, it transpired, had been despatched from Louth, although a decision was subsequently taken to bring the patient to the larger hospital at Lincoln rather than the nearer one where the ambulance was based.

Armed with the names, Swift rang Louth ambulance depot. One of the two from the crew was on holiday; the other was about to finish his shift but agreed to talk to Swift at his home provided it could be done quickly, as he had been on a long shift and needed some sleep.

Swift was beginning to get the hang of blaring a trail across the Lincolnshire Wolds, on this occasion cutting across in roughly a straight line from Wragby to Louth rather than following the main road in a south easterly curve through Horncastle.

Derek White was still in his ambulance uniform when Swift arrived.

"No point in getting changed," he said. "I'm going straight to bed as soon as we've finished. I'm dead beat so can we please make this as short as possible?"

Swift nodded her assent.

"I'll come straight to the point, then," she said. "I'm informed that you were one of a two-man ambulance crew who picked up a man called Oscar Dover at an address in Willoughby Road, Alford, a couple of weeks ago.

"He had collapsed. You took him to Lincoln County Hospital. You may remember it because I gather there was some debate whether he should go to Lincoln or Louth, which was nearer."

White's mouth opened at the same time as Swift's, but in his case it was an ill concealed yawn. Half way through the detective sergeant's short spiel, however, White stifled the yawn and started paying attention. He clearly remembered the case so there was no point in denying it.

"Yeah, yeah," he said vaguely. "I think I know who you're

on about. If it's who I think you mean, we got there within the target time and he was still alive when we handed him over at the hospital. What's the problem?"

"His sister, Stella Dover, was with him at the house," Swift said, ignoring the question.

"Yeah, yeah, there was some woman there," White said wearily. "I don't think she came in the ambulance though. Look, I'm very tired. It will all be in the report."

"It's not what's in the report that interests me," Swift said. "It's what's not in it."

"Can we please stop playing games. I'm too tired for games. You said you were coming straight to the point."

"Did Stella Dover tell you what she thought was wrong with her brother?"

"She said he'd collapsed. She said he'd had heart trouble in the past. I told them at the hospital."

"Did she also tell you that she believed that someone had poisoned her brother?"

White fell silent. He was struggling with the questions in the face of overwhelming tiredness. Swift pressed her advantage, but not too quickly. The longer the questioning continued, the less resistance White would be able to summon up.

"It's a simple enough question, Mr White," Swift said eventually. "You surely would remember something like that. Did she say she thought her brother had been poisoned?"

"Well, she did, but…" White began.

"And did you mention it to anyone at the hospital?" Swift demanded.

"Well, no but…"

"Why not? It could have saved his life."

"Because," White said, suddenly fighting back, "because I didn't take her seriously. And I still don't. She didn't mention it at first. It was only when we'd got him in the ambulance and my partner was radioing in that she mentioned it.

"She suddenly got all hysterical and started raving about him being poisoned. People always think they know better than you what is wrong and what you should be doing. I calmed her down as best I could. She was holding us up. If we'd stayed there arguing the toss with her he'd have been dead before we left the house."

"Did Stella Dover ask to come in the ambulance with her brother?"

"No. I assumed she would be doing but she suddenly rushed up the path into the house and slammed the door shut behind her. There wasn't time to chase after her. Oscar Dover's pulse was weak, his heart rate was down, we feared his heart was packing up.

"That's why we came to Lincoln rather than Louth. They're more geared up to deal with this kind of case – heart attacks, I mean."

"Did you mention the possibility of poisoning in any report?"

"Of course not. We're already bogged down with enough paperwork as it is. Putting something like that when I didn't believe she meant it anyway would simply have added to the bureaucracy. There'd have been a witch hunt and it wouldn't have saved him so what was the point?"

Chapter 7

David was proving remarkably adept at organising the new Amos-led department. Years of running round desperately following the Chief Constable's bidding had inevitably honed his skills. Being distanced from Sir Robert, if only temporarily, gave him an unaccustomed freedom.

"I'll organise the schools if you draw up the roster of police officers," he said with a firmness he would not have dared to confront Sir Robert Fletcher with. Having Sir Robert's authority to deal with Amos was a vital morale boost for the press officer.

"Yes, okay," Amos said without enthusiasm, although he was conscious that the more David took on the less hassle it would be for himself.

"Good idea," he said suddenly, brightening up. "I'll tackle the Lincolnshire Echo and the local BBC people."

David looked up in alarm. Liaison with the press was his responsibility. Letting Amos loose with journalists tended to have a disastrous effect.

"Yes, I know," Amos said hastily, "I know it's your job but you heard Sir Robert. He told me to use my contacts to get publicity for the project."

David looked dubious as Amos rang Sheila Burns, his main contact at the Echo, and arranged to meet her for coffee at their usual haunt near the Stonebow in Lincoln city centre in an hour's time. He used the intervening time to fix a slot the following morning on the 11am chat show on Radio Lincolnshire and to make contact with the regional BBC and commercial TV stations, who promised to get back to him.

Burns was quite enthusiastic about the story.

"Front page lead tomorrow," she assured Amos, "as long as you're sure no-one else will have it first. It's a bit late to give it a decent show today. Deadlines get earlier and earlier and two editions have already gone to press."

Amos said he was quite certain no-one else would have the story before his appearance on the local radio station at 11am on the same morning. Burns was content.

The inspector did not rush back to police HQ. Instead, he went home for lunch with his wife. When he returned to face David, the press officer was in an upbeat mood. Several schools had expressed an interest in taking part.

Calendar, the early evening regional news show on ITV, had rung back asking Amos to get in touch. He did so immediately.

The researcher was as enthusiastic as Sheila Burns had been. Amos felt a mixture of relief that the project was rolling and irritation that he could not share the enthusiasm. David, in contrast, had cast aside his initial fears about working closely with Amos and was taken in by the inspector's apparent commitment to the cause.

"Can we get a school to play ball tomorrow?" Amos asked David as he put down the phone. "Calendar will come and film us talking to the pupils."

David beamed.

"There are two or three possibilities," he said, bringing over a small pile of papers.

Amos glanced at the names of the schools. He was going to pick one in Lincoln as being most convenient until another prospect caught his eye. It was the school that Stella Dover's younger niece attended. He recognised the name from the school badge that he had observed when he and DS Swift had visited the two sisters.

"Let's try this one," the inspector said brightly. "It's a bit more rural than Lincoln so they're more likely to be willing to accommodate us at short notice. I don't suppose they get much media attention.

"I'll give them a ring myself," he added hastily as David made to take back the paper bearing the details. One school was as good as another for the purposes of the project and it was just possible, however unlikely, that something would come to light that would help Det Sgt Swift's inquiry into Oscar Dover's death.

Amos dialled the number quickly as David hovered nervously. It was a pleasant surprise for the Chief Constable's press secretary to hear the headmaster of the school getting the hard sell. Amos finally put the phone down with an air of satisfaction.

"It seems that this project fits nicely into some new-fangled GCSE course about citizenship," Amos said. "He's going to round-up all those taking the exam this year and we can talk to them in the afternoon. It gives us a great angle for the television slot."

David beamed, then his face suddenly darkened.

"But who's going to do it?" he wailed. "We haven't got a speaking team together yet. We haven't got anyone briefed on what to say."

"No problem," Amos declared emphatically. "I will naturally take the lead myself. I can easily get there in time after doing the radio interview in the morning. I need to know what this task demands, so I can lead the team properly, and how to make the best use of the opportunity to take policing out into the community."

The inspector surprised even himself with his breathtaking hypocrisy. What he really wanted to do was snaffle all the publicity for himself. Why shouldn't he? It would make up for the tedium of being sidelined in this dead end job.

It took only a couple of minutes to commandeer the services of a uniformed constable to accompany him. The threat of retribution from the Chief Constable was sufficient incentive.

Amos and PC John Lowe arrived at the school in good time for the session due to start at 2pm. Even so, the Calendar team was already setting up their lighting, camera and microphone.

The headmaster took Amos on one side.

"I could only get three of this year's exam takers in," he said urgently. "We let them study at home in the run-up to exams so it was a bit difficult. I've roped in the next year down to make up the numbers. Is that all right?"

"Perfectly in order," Amos said generously. "As long as we have a roomful no-one will know any different. Let's just keep this to ourselves, shall we."

The headmaster was only too happy to exercise discretion.

"The exam year are rather a difficult lot," he confided. "Most of them will leave as soon as they've finished their GCSEs and I shan't be too sorry to see them go."

Amos chuckled.

"It's a pity they'll miss the talk, then," he said. "Sounds like they need it."

Secretly, he was rather pleased not to have to face an unruly class for the first session of the project, especially with a television camera present.

"They certainly do," the head replied ruefully. "We've had a lot of graffiti. The girls are worse than the boys. You should see the obscenities on the walls of the girls' toilets. I was shocked. We'll have to get it painted over in the summer holidays."

Amos tut-tutted in sympathy.

"Then there's the pilfering."

"Have you reported it?" Amos asked.

"No point," came the reply. "They only do it for devilment. It's never worth anything very much and we'd never be able to catch the culprits. No-one's going to snitch. The only time it was ever an issue was a couple of years ago when some stuff got nicked from the chemistry lab. Don't worry, we tightened up after that. Everything is under lock and key now."

"What went missing from the chemistry lab?" Amos asked as casually as he could.

"Oh, nothing serious," the headmaster said hastily, regretting his indiscretion. "Just some powder. Only a few grams. I'm not sure what – I'm an arts man myself – but the chemistry master promised it wouldn't harm anyone."

At this point a couple of pupils wandered in and started getting in the way of the TV crew. The headmaster promptly excused himself and started to fuss round ostentatiously, causing amusement among the growing number of pupils filtering in.

Soon the lure of an appearance on the telly overcame the pleasure of taunting the headmaster and calm prevailed as Amos stepped up to launch the grand project in front of a decent sized audience. The session went better than the inspector dared to hope, despite one or two lusty interruptions.

It was only at the end, when the TV crew was losing interest anyway as they had enough in the can, that the really awkward moment cropped up.

"Is it true you're investigating Lynn's Uncle Oscar?" one of the boys suddenly piped up.

Amos quickly erased the shock from his face.

"I can't possibly comment on an individual," he said uncertainly. "I can tell you that a police officer is attached to the coroner's court and every sudden death is investigated. The vast majority turn out to be natural causes."

"My Mum says you are," the boy said with a smirk on his face. "And I'm not talking about him dying. I'm talking about what he got up to."

Fortunately the crew were now packing up and showing no interest in the exchange.

"Well, it's a good job I don't have to answer to your Mum," Amos said testily. "I answer to the Chief Constable. In any case, everyone in this country is assumed to be innocent until they are found guilty in a court of law. So unless he was found guilty of anything he was an innocent man."

"My Mum said he was a dirty old man," the pupil persisted. "She said I wasn't to go anywhere near him. He collects pictures of naked boys. Or he did. He's dead now and my Mum says good riddance."

"Your Mum has a lot to say for herself," Amos said coolly as he tried to disguise his interest in this unexpected information. "Tell your Mum that if she has any information of law breaking she should take it to the police."

The headmaster has keen to usher Amos out of the room as quickly as possible before the wretched boy made any more wild assertions.

"I assume you'd rather I get his name and address from your records rather than from the boy himself," Amos remarked casually once they were out into the corridor.

The head looked disappointed.

"Do you really need to pursue this?" he asked anxiously.

"Boys say all sorts of things. You mustn't take too much notice. In any case, he said the person concerned is dead so what's the point of bothering?"

"Nevertheless," Amos persisted, "I shall need his details. We may feel that in all the circumstances we should inquire further. I can't say at this stage."

This was not strictly true. Amos knew perfectly well that Det Sgt Swift would almost certainly want to talk to the boy's mother.

At that point the pupils started to file out. Amos opened his mouth as if to speak to the boy who had made the accusation.

"Yes, yes, of course," the head said quickly. "Naturally we would always cooperate with the police."

He led the way to his study and ordered his secretary to dig out the required information.

Once this had been safely acquired, Amos added: "And the chemistry teacher. I just need a quick word with him."

The headmaster's face turned white but he made no protest.

"His name is Tim Armstrong," he said. "You'll find him in the chemistry lab. Please could I ask you not to cause a stir among the pupils. They are difficult enough as it is and if they think that what they tell you is taken seriously it could all get out of hand."

"Discretion is my middle name," Amos replied.

The inspector followed the headmaster's directions to the chemistry lab. Thanks to the lax arrangements that allowed pupils to study at home, the chemistry master was alone in his domain.

Amos introduced himself.

"I hear you're giving pep talks on good citizenship," Armstrong remarked guardedly.

"I understand they may be needed," Amos replied smoothly. "I gather things go missing."

Armstrong looked uncomfortable.

"So I understand," he said without conviction.

"And I understand," Amos said firmly, "that a substance went missing from the chemistry lab."

"I thought that was where we were heading," Armstrong

said. "It was nothing, I can assure you."

"It's a long time since I was at school," Amos said caustically, "but as far as I recall most of the stuff in the chemistry lab was potentially dangerous. Have things changed?"

Armstrong said nothing.

"So what was nicked?" Amos persisted.

"It was a tiny amount of barium hydroxide. And no, it isn't as horrendous as it sounds. It's an alkali. It's used to test paint pigments."

Amos had not starred at chemistry but he vaguely remembered that acids were corrosive and alkalis were the opposite.

"When did it go missing?" he asked.

"Ages ago," Armstrong said.

"Three or four years ago," he added hastily as Amos looked dissatisfied with so vague an answer. "Three years ago. It was just after the exams. Probably the A level group thinking they were beyond discipline."

"They probably were," Amos agreed.

Amos returned to the police car parked in a section of tarmac allocated to teachers and visitors. He had sent PC John Lowe on ahead immediately the session with the pupils had ended. Only now did it occur to the inspector that Lowe would be getting bored sitting waiting in the car with no idea what was keeping Amos.

Dispatching Lowe was, however, probably a wise move. Far from sitting stewing, Lowe was busy keeping half a dozen boys at bay. Left to their own devices they might well have inflicted damage on the police car.

As Amos approached they diverted their attention to him.

"You going to talk to Teddy's mum?" one boy jeered.

"It's your civic duty," another one taunted Amos.

"Stand clear," Amos said sternly. "It's my civic duty not to run you down."

He got into the driver's seat. Lowe had already extricated himself from the gaggle of schoolboys and was walking round to the passenger side, trying not to look as if he was retreating.

The boys stood back but they followed the police car as it headed slowly for the school gate.

"Sorry to put you through that," Amos told Lowe. "I just wanted to buttonhole the head to get his reaction to the session."

The inspector almost blushed at this blatant and unnecessary lie. He did not have to explain himself to a junior officer, and a uniformed one at that. However, he was keen that no-one other than himself and Swift knew about the probable fool's errand that was the inquiry into the death of Oscar Dover.

"I hope he was happy. I thought it went rather well," Lowe responded. "Do tell the Chief Constable if you get chance – but don't be too enthusiastic or I'll be stuck with it for the duration."

"I'm happy to put in a word for you," Amos said, "but in return would you please try to keep out of his and David's way when we get back. I want a word with Juliet Swift before bracing myself for the ascent to the top floor."

They completed the journey back to HQ in silence. DS Swift was at her desk, trying to look busy but succeeding only in looking bored when Amos entered CID.

"Come into my office, Juliet," he said trying not to look at Jennifer. The Oscar Dover business was for his and Swift's ears only.

Cocooned in the office with the door closed, Swift spoke first.

"You won't be surprised to hear that I'm not really getting anywhere, Sir," she said. "There's only one real suspect and she doesn't have any reason to kill her own brother. And there's no evidence even if she did."

"I may have discovered another side to Oscar Dover's character that might be worth investigating even if he died a natural death," Amos replied.

They were seated either side of Amos's desk. Swift sat up with a start.

"It could make it worth pursuing the matter even if there's no chance of catching a murderer. At least it gives you a decent excuse to press on if you want to. It seems that our late unlamented friend Oscar may have been a pervert."

Swift gasped.

"It's only hearsay and probably full of schoolboy exaggeration," Amos went on, "but according to a boy called Teddy Grantham, Oscar Dover kept pictures of naked boys in his wallet. His mother told him to stay well clear. I got the impression his mother knows quite a bit about Dover's proclivities."

"I've never understood how men who fancy young boys manage to get married and have children," Swift said, "but I know it happens. You'd think the wives would cotton on."

"As you say, it happens," Amos said. "Oscar Wilde was married with two children. It's a way of looking respectable."

He handed over a piece of paper with the name and address of Grantham's mother.

"As far as I can gather from the school records she doesn't have a job so you've a good chance of catching her at home if you want to follow it up. It's your call."

"I'll go and see her tomorrow," Swift said. "It's better than getting dragged into petty stuff, which is what will happen if I hang around here. I'll take my chance on her being in. Besides, I'd rather try to catch her off guard than warn her I'm coming. "

Amos wandered back upstairs to his new office to find David jumping up and down.

"We were front page lead in the Echo," the press secretary enthused. "We're on Calendar tonight. Sir Robert is delighted."

Not too delighted I hope, Amos thought to himself.

He and David sorted out some more school visits and allocated officers. It was only later that he realised had had forgotten to mention to Swift about the missing chemical. It probably wasn't important. It was apparently harmless stuff and it was taken quite some time ago.

Chapter 8

Young Teddy Grantham had been unexpectedly vociferous about the alleged proclivities of Oscar Dover; his mother Nadine was surprisingly reluctant.

Detective Sergeant Juliet Swift approached her house in high hopes that at last she would be talking to someone with a genuine interest in providing much needed background detail on the man who might or might not have been murdered. The problem, she expected, would be to restrict the woman to facts and weed out wild speculation.

When Swift introduced herself on the doorstep and showed her warrant card, Nadine Grantham staggered back as if hit by a thunderbolt, grabbing the dado rail down the hall wall for support.

"No please," she gasped to Swift's astonishment. "Please, not Teddy. Please tell me it's not Teddy."

Swift stepped forward and grasped the woman's free hand.

"Teddy's not in any trouble, Mrs Grantham," Swift said, misunderstanding the cause of her distress.

"Nothing's happened to him?" Grantham said pleadingly. "He's not had an accident?"

"No," Swift said reassuringly. "He's fine."

Grantham was still badly shaken. Swift helped her through into her lounge and into a comfortable armchair.

"I couldn't think what else it could be," the woman said apologetically.

Swift was soon to realise that the misunderstanding was a stroke of luck. She would probably not have got through the door without it.

"We're running a schools project at the moment, with officers talking to pupils," Swift said. "I'm not taking part in it myself but your son made comments to one of my colleagues which we felt we had to investigate. I understand that you warned him about a man called Oscar Dover from Alford."

"I can't think what on earth he could have said to your colleague," Grantham blustered. "I hardly knew the man."

"But you did know him?" Swift persisted.

"Well, I knew of him."

"He lived not far away at one time, I believe. Did you know him here?"

Grantham nodded.

"Mrs Grantham," Swift said in exasperation. "You must have known him. Why else would you tell your son to stay away from him?"

Grantham sat in silence for a few moments, weighing up the situation. Swift was in no rush. However, it was she who finally broke the silence.

"You're aware that he died recently?" Swift asked, more as a statement than a question.

Again, Grantham nodded.

"Look," she suddenly blurted out, "you shouldn't take any notice of Teddy. Teenage boys get things all out of proportion. I just warned him about the real world, that's all. He doesn't have a dad for a role model."

"But you warned him specifically about Oscar Dover," Swift protested. "You must have had a reason."

Grantham merely shrugged her shoulders.

"How do you know what he had in his wallet?" Swift persisted.

This visibly rattled the woman.

"What do you mean?"

"You know he had photographs in his wallet. Now how did you know that?"

"It was just a figure of speech," Grantham protested unconvincingly.

"No it wasn't," Swift pressed her advantage. Then a thought occurred to her.

"Did he have a photograph of you?" she asked quietly.

Grantham sank into a chair, collapsed over the table and burst into tears. She sobbed uncontrollable for what seemed like eternity to Swift, who really didn't know what to do.

Finally, Grantham nodded.

"Was he Teddy's father?" Swift asked.

"Yes," Grantham said. "Don't tell me I was stupid. I know that already. I've no idea what I saw in him. He had no attractive features at all."

Swift now felt sympathy. She had no idea why she was with her boyfriend Jason, who was a waste of space at the best of times and was probably having an affair despite all the support she had given him over the years. Why were the nicest women always attracted to the worst blokes?

"He was on bad terms with his wife," Grantham said, apparently now anxious to get it all off her chest. "He promised me we would be together. Can you believe I was stupid enough to believe him? Can you believe I was stupid enough to let him take a nude picture of me?

"Of course he was soon fed up of me once he'd got what he wanted."

"But why did you tell Teddy he had pictures of boys?"

"Because he did. The last time he came round I could tell he was losing interest in me. I feared the worst if I couldn't get the photo back. He left his jacket over the chair when he went to the toilet so I took my chance to get his wallet and retrieve my picture.

"Except my picture wasn't there. But there *were* disgusting pictures of underage boys. I was so shocked I just stood there. He came back, snatched the wallet out of my hand and stormed off. Not before warning me, though, that if I ever breathed a word about it everyone I knew would see my photograph.

"So I kept quiet and hoped for the best. As far as I know he never showed anyone my picture. At least no-one ever said. I never saw him again."

"So why warn Teddy about him?"

"Because one day Teddy came home and said there had been trouble outside the school. Some older boys had been hanging around the school gates but Lynn Dover's father had come and spoken to them and they'd cleared off.

"Everyone was asking Lynn what his secret power was. They couldn't believe a little weed like him could face down a group of strapping lads. They all thought it was great.

"I didn't. I was horrified. It was the first time he had ever mention this Lynn Dover so I had no idea Oscar had a daughter at the same school. Of course, Teddy didn't know he and Lynn shared the same father. But I had to warn him off just in case Oscar came round the school again.

"Please don't tell Teddy who his father was. I hope he never finds out."

Chapter 9

There were two cafes in Alford market place, which was a bit inconvenient, but only one had a couple of tables outside where Oscar Dover could have sat on fine days watching Alford go by.

It was past breakfast time but too early for lunch, so the café was empty apart from a middle-aged woman who was clearing tables inside and going over the table tops with a cursory wipe of a damp grey cloth.

Det Sgt Swift realised that word might have reached the café about her interest in the death of Oscar Dover. After all, the man had frequented the establishment and Stella Dover lived just down the road. Swift decided, therefore, not to extend the subterfuge of making casual inquiries. Instead, she introduced herself formally.

The woman gave her name as Janet Templeton, then she switched the hot water urn back on without bothering to ask Swift if she wanted a brew.

"Fire away," she said cheerfully as she placed tea bags into two beakers. "Toast?"

Swift nodded. It would make the interview more like a cosy chat, which might have its advantages.

Templeton stuck four pieces of sliced bread into the toaster. Swift looked away to hide her distaste for processed bread. By now the urn, which had apparently not cooled off too far since the breakfast run, was up to boiling point and Templeton put the beakers under the tap in turn and filled them.

To Swift's disgust, the woman took a carton of milk from the fridge, unscrewed the top and poured a generous amount into the two beakers before the tea bags had turned the water to a golden brown.

"I'm making some discreet inquiries about a man called Oscar Dover," Swift began while Templeton was still fishing the toast out of the toaster. She didn't want to rush but you never knew if a customer would come in and break up the chat.

"I believe he was a customer of yours."

Templeton raised her eyebrows.

"Yes, Ossie came in quite a lot," she said absentmindedly as she put the plates of toast and butter onto the counter. "Marmalade?"

Fearful that the quality of the marmalade would be less than optimum, Swift declined. As Templeton transferred the tea and toast to the table, she added: "He didn't spend much. A mug of tea went a long way with him. Still, I was sorry to hear he had passed away. It was a bit of a shock, being so sudden and all. I didn't even know about it until I remarked to someone that I hadn't seen him lately."

"Would you describe him as a friend?" Swift asked.

Templeton screwed her face up as if thinking of the answer was a real quandary.

"I wouldn't say that," she answered. "In fact, I'm not sure he had any friends. Not real friends. I knew of him around the town, of course, like everybody else. I knew his sister Stella better and for longer, though she was a bit of a funnyosity, sometimes greeting you like a long-lost buddy and other times she seemed she hardly wanted to know you.

"Ossie ran an antiques shop, for want of a better word. Junk shop more like. Full of other people's furniture and knickknacks. I picked up a few pieces cheap for the café when I was setting up. Some of these chairs came from him – and a couple of tables. The clock on the wall over there," she added with a wave in its direction.

"He always asked for too much," Templeton said, "but you could always knock him down to a decent price. The trick was to catch him when he'd just got another delivery and he needed to make space. If you knew what to offer you could do all right."

"You surprise me," Swift said, hastily swallowing a large piece of toast that she had greedily bitten off while Templeton was talking. The plastic bread tasted better than expected coming so long after her last decent meal.

"I thought he did rather well from selling stuff that he'd picked up cheaply."

"You don't want to believe all you hear," Templeton said with a forced laugh. "He always made out he was doing well but it was all show. If he was doing that well he could have afforded more than one cup of tea an hour. He could make one tea last all morning."

Templeton seemed to have forgotten she was technically being interviewed by a police officer. She was treating the episode like a pleasant chat with an old friend. Loneliness is a great virtue in an interviewee, Swift thought to herself.

"Perhaps other people took it at face value and thought he'd gained at their expense?" she said aloud.

"Well, there was that," Templeton conceded, sipping her tea. "Some people did have a go at him. He used to sit outside unless it was raining, even when it was cold and he had to sit in his coat. Once or twice people he'd rubbed up the wrong way would have a caustic word or two with him but they generally gave up when they realised he took no notice."

"He didn't hide away in a corner, then," Swift ventured. "I would have done if people were cross with me."

"I really don't think he cared all that much, at least not towards the end. He became a sad old man. By then hardly anybody spoke to him. He just sat out there, staring into space."

"Did you know his daughter Julia?" Swift asked.

Templeton shook her head.

"I don't think so," she said doubtfully.

"Tall girl, dark hair, early 20s."

A light dawned on Templeton's face.

"I bet that was the girl he was sitting with just before he died," she said triumphantly. "I wondered who it was. I was so surprised. He'd ordered a tea as usual and was sitting outside on his own. A bit later I looked out of the window and there was this young woman sitting on the opposite side of the table."

"Did you go out to them?" Swift asked eagerly. "How did they seem?"

"They were just talking," Templeton said. "I can't say what about."

"Did they look animated?" Swift persisted. "Were they having a row?"

"I don't think so," Templeton said. "I don't really know. There were only two of us working in the café, one cooking and me serving and I had people to attend to first. By the time I got round to going out to see what she wanted to order she'd got up and was walking off.

"I watched her stride across the road and get into a car without so much as a backward glance. Ossie was just sitting there staring into his mug. As soon as she'd driven away he got up and walked off himself."

"I hope he'd paid for his cuppa," Swift remarked lightly.

Templeton's reaction to this innocent remark was out of all proportion. She leapt up without directly answering the question, grabbed hold of the plates and beakers and stomped off behind the counter to stack the crockery noisily into the dishwasher, running a serious risk of breaking something.

Somewhat disconcerted, Swift wandered back to her car. It was only later that she wondered if she should have offered to pay for her tea and toast.

Chapter 10

Det Sgt Juliet Swift decided to follow the old police maxim:
If all else fails, try the local pub. She selected the hostel that
was within striking distance of both the house that Stella and
Oscar Dover had shared and the lock-up where Oscar had kept
the various items that he had bought before selling them on.

It was hardly lunchtime but a couple of men in their fifties
were already present, sitting on bar stools with a pint of beer
each in front of them and leaning across to chat to the
landlord. That was an ideal number, enough to stand a chance
that someone would be able and willing to help but not so
many to destroy the atmosphere of a cosy chat.

The desultory buzz of conversation ceased as Swift walked
in as casually as she could manage. Three pairs of eyes turned
on her. It was still unusual for a lone woman to enter a public
house, especially so early in the day.

Swift ordered a pint of shandy. It limited her alcohol intake
safely below the legal driving limit, whereas asking for a non-
alcoholic drink would have put a barrier between her and the
other drinkers. Swift wanted ideally to edge into the
conversation without creating too much attention, then steer it
round to the subject of Oscar Dover as gently as possible.

It was a pretty tall order in a pub that bore the hallmarks of a
men's refuge. The room was pretty spartan. The tables and
chairs were wooden and basic. A dartboard was all that hung
on the wall. It struck Swift that women didn't frequent the
place at all, unaccompanied or otherwise.

"Are you from round here, Miss?" the landlord asked
pleasantly as he more than half filled the pint glass with
lemonade. "I don't think we've seen you in here before."

He knows perfectly well he hasn't seen me in here before,
Swift said to herself. However, it gave her the excuse to slide
onto one of the unoccupied bar stools.

"No, and no," she replied as the landlord removed the end of the beer spout to dampen the effervescence created as beer plunged into lemonade. "I'm not from round here, so no, I've not been in before."

She decided on the spur of the moment to take the bull by the horns as the landlord placed the shandy in front of her and took a £5 note from her outstretched hand. It was clear that they had not realised she was a police officer.

"I'm trying to track down Uncle Oscar," she said. "Oscar Dover. I believe he lived somewhere near here. Do you by any chance know him?"

The three men clearly did know Oscar Dover. One drinker emitted a low whistle; the other stopped downing his ale in mid gulp and put his glass back on the bar; the landlord paused with the till open and the fiver still in his hand. The three men looked at each other.

"Your uncle, was he?" the landlord said after a few seconds.

He put the five pound note into the till and selected Swift's change.

"I'm sorry, love," the landlord continued. "There's no easy way to say this. I'm afraid you're too late. Ossie's dead."

Swift did not feign surprise or shock. One deceit was sufficient. She had learnt long ago that the fewer falsehoods you perpetrate the less trouble you ultimately have extricating yourself.

"It's all right," she said with quiet resignation and a mixture of fact and fantasy. "We weren't close, as you could imagine. Otherwise I wouldn't be asking where he lived. I'm just looking into the family."

"Doing a family tree, are you?" one of the customers guessed. "His sister lives down Willoughby Road. Stella Dover, she's called. They lived together so she should be able to tell you anything you want to know."

"We never see her in here," the second customer remarked.

I'm not surprised Swift thought. Out loud, she said: "Does that mean Oscar came in? It sounds like you knew him."

The three men glanced at each other uncertainly.

"He came in, yes," the landlord said guardedly. "But not often and he kept pretty much to himself."

"He got very secretive towards the end," one customer added.

Swift put on an air of puzzlement.

Again, the three men present exchanged glances as if unsure whether to say more. The damsel-in-distress look that Swift effected won over the customer nearest to her.

"Look," he said, "Ossie used to be good company in the old days but he got more and more withdrawn after he came back to live with his sister. He'd been married and I think he had children. I seem to remember him talking about his daughter – or was it daughters plural? – when he first came back. I think his marriage broke up."

"Didn't his wife die?" the other customer butted in. "I'm sure that's what he said."

"Well, it doesn't matter," the first customer said testily. "He was pretty cut up either way. Then he started falling out with people over the junk shop he ran. People complained he was ripping them off and he got very off-hand with them.

"It got at the end that no-one would go anywhere near him," the other customer interrupted once more to the annoyance of his fellow drinker.

"Well, if you want to tell her, tell her about the parcels you used to deliver to his junk shop. Never addressed to his home, were they? He kept them well away from sister Stella's prying eyes."

The room fell silent again at this truculent response.

"Parcels?" Swift asked with innocent curiosity.

"Parcels," the first customer repeated. "Jim's a postman. He knows about the parcels."

"You'll get me into trouble," the man called Jim said sullenly.

"It's between us," Swift said firmly. "It won't go any further. It really would help me to learn as much as I can."

"Well, it's no secret," Jim said, "even if no decent minded people talk about it in public. Oscar Dover got in with some pretty bad people. I'm sorry you had to learn this about your uncle.

"Some people don't know when to keep their mouths shut,"

he added accusingly to his drinking companion.

"Please don't fall out on my account," Swift said hastily. "Like I say, I wasn't close to him. You'd better tell me what was going on so I'm prepared if anyone else mentions it – as they are likely to do."

"Ossie started making enemies," the first drinker said. "He had a junk shop but he sold all the better stuff through auction houses. A lot of people felt cheated by him. He paid peanuts for stuff he knew was valuable and then sold it for a fortune. People started talking to each other. Then they stopped talking to him."

"So these parcels you mentioned were stuff he'd bought?" Swift asked.

"I don't like to talk about these things with a young lady," Jim said. "It isn't right. But no, they were not about his junk. They were photographs. Nude photographs. They were disgusting. Some were of children. I'm sorry love, I hope I haven't shocked or offended you."

"Did you see these pictures?" Swift asked. "Are you sure?"

"I didn't open the envelopes, if that's what you mean," the man said indignantly.

"Of course not. I didn't mean to imply that," Swift said hastily, though he must have seen inside the envelopes if he knew their content. "But it's a lot to take in. You say he fell in with a bad lot. Who were these people?"

"We don't really know them. They don't live in Alford. They're not the sort of people to make themselves known. But everybody knows there's a ring of perverts. They circulate stuff among themselves."

"Remember when you delivered a package to the Dragon's Den, Jim?" the unnamed customer remarked with a chuckle. "Course you do. It wasn't that long ago."

Jim started to splutter and rise from his seat. His companion closed his mouth abruptly and turned back to his drink.

"Your uncle fell in with a bad lot," Jim repeated. "They could be very intimidating. It was best to keep well clear of them."

Swift decided there was no point in persisting with a line of conversation that had probably unearthed as much information as it was going to do, but she didn't want to switch to asking about the junk business too abruptly.

The landlord mistook the pause for scepticism.

"It does you credit, love," he said patronisingly, "that you don't want to believe us. I was dubious myself at first. But Oscar mixed with some funny types. We all knew what they were up to, even if the police never did anything about it.

"I think living with his sister drove him crackers. Well, it isn't natural, is it, brother and sister sharing a home."

"Even his daughters disowned him," one of the customers said. "Threw him out, they did. That's how he ended up living with sister Stella."

Swift nodded as if taking in all that had been said.

"Where was his junk shop?" she asked. "In Alford?"

"Near the market square," the landlord replied quickly, relieved to be moving away from the less desirable and potentially explosive topic of pornographic photographs.

"He kept a pile of stuff in the lock-up behind it. I wouldn't fancy sifting through that lot," he added with a forced laugh.

"He must have left a lot of money," Swift said injudiciously.

"What's this about, Miss?" the landlord asked sharply. "Are you gold digging?"

Seeing three pairs of hostile eyes turned on her, Swift downed the rest of her shandy and left without another word.

She called in at police HQ on her long slow way home. Her boyfriend Jason, so often out of work, was for once in gainful employment, though how long it would last she was unwilling to think about. In the meantime she was in no rush to return to an empty house.

The detective sergeant was surprised to find Amos in CID, looking like a lost soul.

"Hello, Juliet," he remarked dolefully. "How goes it? I hope Jason isn't going to blame me for your late arrival home."

Swift gave him a wan smile. On several occasions during periods of unemployment Jason had indeed turned up at HQ and berated Amos for the long and irregular hours that Swift, in common with other detectives including Amos, sometimes had to work.

"He's in work," Swift said with a bitter tone. "I don't know which is worse, having him under my feet or not knowing where he is."

The room was empty apart from the two of them. Swift suddenly sank into a chair, her head in her hands. She was close to tears.

"I think he's having an affair. He's always late home from work and he makes up cock-and-bull stories about working overtime and wanting to make a good impression. It's never bothered him in any of his previous jobs. He's very evasive but I can't risk backing him into a corner because I've gone on at him often enough to pull himself together and make an effort."

The thought of Swift's boyfriend having an affair surprised Amos, who held Jason in pretty low regard. What on earth would any woman see in him? He had no idea what attraction he had for a charming, outgoing, vibrant young woman such as Juliet Swift.

"He absolutely dotes on you," Amos said firmly. "He'd be out of his mind to play away."

The inspector realised too late that this was an unfortunate turn of phrase. Jason was a Rugby Union player. He had the physical attraction that Swift lacked. She was the one blessed with personality. They made a contrasting couple.

Swift was also made of sterner stuff than Jason. However humiliating it was at times to live with him, it was even more humiliating to blubber over the prospect of losing him to another woman. She quickly recovered her composure.

"Don't you have a home to go to, either?" she asked.

Amos shrugged his shoulders.

"I just came down here to keep in touch with reality," he said.

"Thanks for the tipoff about what you heard at the school," Swift said. "I've just been told that Oscar Dover received packages containing pornographic images, including those of children. I've no more hard evidence than you have, but two separate reports pointing in the same direction is too much of a coincidence.

"I think I'll ask for a search warrant tomorrow morning and see what I can find in his junk shop. You don't think I should go back tonight, do you?"

"It'll wait until the morning," Amos agreed. "Take Susan Smith with you. She's at a bit of a loose end at the moment. I wish I could come with you myself but I will still be working on a higher plane."

The inspector looked upwards to indicate the top floor of the building where an uneasy truce prevailed between himself and David.

Chapter 11

Early next morning Swift was knocking at the home of Miss Woodward, the Justice of the Peace who lived closest to Lincolnshire Police Headquarters.

Swift had finally decided against taking precipitate action the previous evening. She was still unsure whether any crime had been committed, since reports of Oscar Dover's murder and his predilection for pornography were entirely unsubstantiated hearsay. Nevertheless, with no real crimes to get her teeth into at HQ, she decided after sleeping on it to take a look at Dover's shop and storeroom.

Woodward had been informed of the detective sergeant's impending visit but she looked surprised as she opened the front door.

"What, no Amos?" she inquired.

It hadn't occurred to Swift how much in the shadow of Paul Amos she had been but this was, indeed, the first time that she had approached Woodward for a search warrant off her own bat.

"Correct," Swift said. "This is my investigation. Detective Inspector Amos is otherwise engaged."

"Caught up in this plot to reform the criminals before they become criminals," Woodward said drily as she showed Swift into her front room, a room familiar to Swift from previous visits alongside Amos. "I'm governor of one of the schools he's been lumbered with. Poor Amos."

Woodward allowed herself a rare smile in the presence of a police officer seeking a search warrant.

Swift explained, on oath, the nature of her inquiry. Her request for a warrant to search not only Oscar Dover's shop and store but also his bedroom was granted only in part.

"You can rummage through his bric-a-brac," Woodward said, "but I can't see any justification for disrupting his sister's home. If you come back from the shop with any genuine leads,

I'll think again."

A few moments later Swift was making the increasingly familiar journey to Alford, this time accompanied by Detective Constable Susan Smith, for whom the ride was something of a novelty, living as she did to the west of Lincoln right on the border with Nottinghamshire.

For once, Swift was in no rush. What she was looking for would be there, if it existed at all, whenever she got there.

It was the best part of an hour later that she found herself knocking on the second door of the day, that of Stella Dover, while Smith remained in the car.

"Didn't think you'd be back," Dover said bluntly. "Have you come to tell me my nieces have seen reason?"

This time she kept Swift on the doorstep.

"It's not to do with your dispute with your nieces," Swift replied coolly. "I have a warrant to search your brother's shop and storeroom."

She produced the piece of paper signed by the JP. Stella Dover took it and turned it over casually in her fingers.

"Hmmph," she said as she handed it back. "And may I ask why? What's this got to do with who owns my house?"

"Like I said, Miss Dover," Swift persisted. "It's nothing to do with your family home. It's a completely different line of inquiry."

"What line of inquiry?" Dover demanded. "Is this anything to do with me saying Oscar had been poisoned? Because if it is I take it all back."

"Evidence has come to light regarding an entirely different and unrelated matter. I'm really not prepared to discuss it on your doorstep. Do you have the key to the shop or do I have to break the door down?"

"Hmmph. Wait here. I'll get it."

Dover shut the door in Swift's face but a few moments later it was opened again and Oscar's sister handed over a ring with several keys attached.

"You don't need me to come with you, I take it," she said. "I've got better things to do."

"That's entirely up to you."

"Please make sure you lock up properly when you've done."

Swift was surprised at the casual response from Stella Dover. However, the officers had already spied out the location of the shop, and the storeroom at the rear, as they did not want to give her the satisfaction of being asked to give directions.

Two minutes later they stood on the pavement outside the premises. The shop to the front was two storeys high, the storeroom to the rear was single storey.

Since there was a letter box in the door of the shop, Swift pushed hard as she entered the premises. She assumed that junk mail would have been piling up behind the door since the death of Stella's brother. She almost fell in to the shop as the door swung open easily.

Various leaflets and circulars had been collected up and left neatly on an old table that was presumably one of the items that Oscar Dover had collected from a house clearance. Some china ornaments stood on this piece of furniture.

So Stella Dover had been in and tidied up a bit. Swift started to feel a sinking sensation.

A fair amount of dust had gathered on the floor and furniture, not just since the shop owner's death but probably over a prolonged period while he was still alive. Tell-tale marks showed that items had been moved recently. Very recently.

In particular, stuff had been moved to allow access to drawers and cabinets.

Swift and Smith worked their way slowly and laboriously through the crowded lower storey, looking in any nooks and crannies as well as inside and underneath furniture. There really was nothing to incriminate Oscar Dover.

A similar story emerged from the crowded storeroom at the rear.

"We might as well try upstairs," Swift said without enthusiasm. The whole pointless exercise was taking even longer than she had expected.

"I think we're far too late. Stella Dover has been here before us protecting her brother's good name."

The upper floor of the shop proved slightly more interesting, however. Swift spotted something hidden down a crack between two heavy items of furniture. It took the concerted efforts of both women to prise the congested furniture apart sufficiently to get at it.

Finally Swift managed to fish out a large envelope with stiff backing. On the front, in red, were the words "Photographs. Do not bend".

It would have been beyond the strength of Stella Dover to retrieve it, though she probably had not spotted it. It made no difference either way. The envelope proved to be another disappointment. It was empty.

Swift wondered why an earth Oscar had brought such heavy items upstairs in the first place. Perhaps someone had helped him to shift them when the storeroom and shop were particularly crowded and he had not got round to moving them back downstairs.

An Amstrad word processor stood on a desk under the window. Dust-free patches on the desk on either side indicated that small square items, the size of floppy disk cassettes, had been removed.

Swift switched on the machine, noting with relief that the supply of electricity had not been disconnected. Amstrad had come up with a big improvement on bog standard word processors that traditionally had only one drive for the mini-cassettes.

The Amstrads had two drives, an A drive for the "disc of the day", essentially the computer programme disc, and a B drive to write on. To Swift's disappointment, she soon discovered that the A disc was present but there was no disc in drive B.

There was nothing that Oscar Dover had actually written. She needed the discs that had clearly been removed quite recently, too recently for dust to have settled on the tell-tale marks.

Smith had meanwhile found a desk drawer containing a pile of papers. This looked to be the last chance of finding anything worthwhile.

The papers were stacked roughly in date order, the most

recent at the top, as if each new missive had been plonked onto the pile.

Swift pulled out the drawer and put it on top of the desk so she could flick through the papers more easily. They went back a couple of years but once again there was nothing obviously incriminating among them.

Meanwhile Smith had discovered a cardboard box rammed in between the far side of the desk and a dressing table. This was only half full and appeared to contain papers from further back.

"It looks as if he just pulled papers out of the bottom of the drawer and dumped them into here when the drawer filled up," Smith remarked. "It doesn't look like he was big on proper paperwork."

"I doubt if there's very much in them," Swift responded, "otherwise sister Stella would have removed them along with anything else incriminating. Still, we'd better check through them just in case and take them back to HQ when we've done."

What the two detectives did find were details of various transactions that Oscar Dover had conducted with buyers and sellers. Swift dictated various names and addresses to Smith, who wrote them down copiously in her notebook.

"I don't see any form of communication with the Inland Revenue," the detective sergeant said sardonically. "I don't think our friend Oscar declared any of his ill-gotten gains."

"None in my pile of papers either," Smith replied. "I'll take this lot down and lock it in the car boot."

Swift handed her the car keys and continued poking around without getting anywhere until Smith returned.

Swift sighed.

"We'll have to pay Stella Dover another visit," she said to Smith. "It'll probably be a complete waste of time. I can't say I'm looking forward to it but it has to be done. Anyway, it's time you met this formidable woman."

Swift glanced at her watch. She was surprised to see it was well into the afternoon. In addition to the hour it took to drive from Lincoln, she and Smith had taken an inordinately long time working their way painstakingly round the stacked premises for precious little reward.

The officers locked up Oscar Dover's premises and quickly made the short journey back to his sister Stella's home.

Stella Dover opened the door but once again made it clear that she was not going to invite the two detectives in.

"Brought reinforcements have you?" she said caustically to Swift. "Where did you find this one? Don't tell me you found her hiding in a cupboard at the shop."

"We have questions for you," Swift said. "We'd rather do it inside."

"I'd rather do it on the doorstep."

"In that case I'd rather do it at police Headquarters."

"I don't think you would," Dover said quietly, calling Swift's bluff. "If you had any cause to take me in you'd have done it sooner."

"Very well, we'll do it on the doorstep," Swift said, trying not to sound as if she was backing down. "It's not _my_ neighbours who'll be listening."

Dover merely stood defiant, her arms folded.

"You've been round to your brother's shop, I see," Swift said.

"Why shouldn't I? I'm going to have to sort it out."

"And did a bit of tidying up while you were there."

"Just moved the junk mail from behind the door."

"It was rather more than that. You removed things. Don't bother denying it. We could see the marks in the dust."

If Stella Dover was disconcerted she gave no sign of it.

"I've just removed odd bits, anything small enough to carry," she said with a sigh. "Anything wrong with that?"

"Yet you didn't remove the junk mail," Swift persisted. "You left that lying on a table right near the door. You did, though, remove some photographs and some computer discs. And you obviously knew what you were doing because you left the only disc with nothing on it."

"So?"

"What was on them?"

"I've no idea. I didn't look at them."

"You didn't look at the photographs?" Swift gasped incredulously. "I don't believe you."

"You can believe what you like," Dover said firmly. "I didn't look at them."

"Well, let's look at them now," Swift said equally firmly.

"That won't be possible," Dover said. "The photographs have gone. Don't bother coming in looking for them. I burnt them."

"And the discs?" Swift asked without much hope.

"They've gone as well. I smashed them up and put them in the dustbin. It was emptied this morning."

"We've taken the papers you deigned to leave behind," Swift said, covering her back in case Dover chose to complain later. "We've left you the junk mail."

Swift handed back the keys to the shop and turned to leave.

"You can check the bin if you want to," Dover said smugly. "It was emptied this morning. It's still out on the pavement."

Chapter 12

DS Swift declined to give Stella Dover the satisfaction of seeing her look into the bin, though she "accidentally" bumped against it as she and DC Susan Smith returned to their car. The bin moved easily. It was clearly empty.

Swift had been denied a warrant to search the house and there was no point in trying again to obtain one. If there was anything left that incriminated Oscar, which was pretty unlikely anyway, Stella would dispose of it by the time the officers could get back.

The detective sergeant was also not going to demean herself by asking Stella Dover the whereabouts of any address on the list that she and Smith had taken from the papers in the shop. Swift drove back into the centre of Alford. She was getting to know the place and she remembered the whereabouts of a town map.

She and Smith were readily able to locate three addresses within easy reach.

Two were well within walking distance. There was no response to their knock at the first and the woman who opened the door at the second said she had moved in recently after the previous owner had died.

There was no rush to get back to HQ so they walked the quarter mile towards Chapel St Leonards to the third house. This time they were in luck. An elderly man admitted to being the person named on the copy of a receipt at Oscar Dover's shop and, on ascertaining where they had found his name and address, he invited them in.

The man waited until they were all seated in his front room before delivering what he thought would be bad news.

"I'm afraid you're a bit too late to be investigating Oscar Dover," he said apologetically. "I believe he died a couple of weeks ago. At least, that's what someone told me in the pub. I'm not quite sure when because I don't get into Alford much these days."

No, you don't get out much, Swift thought. You are unshaven, such hair as you have left hasn't been combed, or indeed cut recently, and your shirt looks as if it could do with a good wash. I doubt very much if you ventured all the way to the café to poison Oscar Dover.

Still, they might as well go through the motions now they were here.

"Did you know Mr Dover well?" Swift asked pleasantly.

"Not really," their host replied. "Everybody knew Ossie but I don't think anyone knew him really well. He cut a very sad and lonely figure by the end."

Just like you, Swift said to herself, but out loud she asked: "What dealings did you have with him and his shop? You must have known him well enough to sell him some stuff, in fact quite a lot of stuff judging from his copy of the receipt that we found on the premises."

"Yes, he bought quite a bit of stuff off me when my wife died. Well, I didn't really need it any more, cluttering up the place. And what would I want with jewellery, anyway? We didn't have an children so there was no one to leave it to."

"Did he give you a fair price?"

"It was a very good price. He told me so himself."

"You didn't get another valuation?"

"Who from? No-one else took stuff. And he came round to your house to collect it to save you the trouble. I just wanted rid."

"So you didn't have any grudge against Mr Dover?" Swift said. She was ready to give up by this stage.

"You've got the wrong Charlie," the man said with a chuckle.

"I beg your pardon?" Swift asked, perplexed. "I wasn't trying to be insulting."

"I'm Charlie Jones," came the reply. "The man you want is Charlie Smethurst. He was the one with the grudge again Ossie. Charlie Smethurst. That's who you want."

DC Smith was already glancing down her list of names and addresses.

"Does he still live on Mablethorpe Road?" she asked.

"That's him," Jones said brightly. "As far as I know he still does. He's the one you want."

Mablethorpe Road was further out from Alford centre. It was easier to walk on to his place rather than go back into town for the car, although it would entail a correspondingly longer walk back after interviewing him.

"Tell you what," DS Swift said to DC Smith, "why don't we walk up to Mr Smethurst's house, then carry on to the windmill. Inspector Amos said they do afternoon tea but we didn't get chance to try it the last time we came. It'll stoke up our energy for the walk back to the car – unless you're in a hurry to get back to Lincoln."

"Don't worry, sarge," Smith said. "It's all good experience. I'm learning a lot."

Swift liked being called "sarge". Some sergeants, especially younger ones, hated it. They thought it was clunky and made them sound old. Swift felt the rank had been hard earned and she was proud of it.

Her pet hate was "ma'am", which she found aging and should be reserved for the dowdiest, most senior police women, of whom there were few.

"I'm afraid you're learning a lot about what not to do," Swift replied with a grimace.

"It's still learning," Smith assured her.

Smethurst lived in a larger house than Jones. He employed a gardener, who was deadheading flowers in the immaculate front garden, a man whom Swift initially assumed, wrongly, to be the homeowner.

The real Charlie Smethurst answered the door. He was better dressed and more alert than Jones, Swift noticed immediately, though he was probably also of retirement age. His wife is still alive, she surmised, this assumption soon proving to be correct.

"It's about Oscar Dover," Swift said.

"You'd better come in," the man replied.

He showed them into a front room occupied by a woman of similar age who hastily switched off the TV, on which she was watching some trashy afternoon programme, with the remote control as they entered.

"This is my wife, Jessie," Smethurst said. "Do sit down."

Then to his wife he added: "These are police officers, dear, asking about Oscar Dover."

"Thanks," Swift said, as she and Smith did as they were bid. "We won't keep you long but I believe you had some dealings with Mr Dover."

"Dealing singular," Smethurst replied genially but firmly. "If he thought he could take me for a mug he had another think coming."

Swift raised her eyebrows.

"I take it this is about his shop," Smethurst said. "I suppose his carryings on have finally caught up with him."

"I don't want to be too specific," Swift improvised, "because I don't want to influence what you say. But would you please tell us about your own dealings – I mean dealing – with him."

Smethurst sank back into his chair and put the tips of his fingers together, making the shape of a house roof, and thought deeply.

"I really don't like telling tales about him," he finally said.

"You should tell them, though dear," his wife said. It was the first utterance she had made since the detectives had entered the room. "He really shouldn't be allowed to get away with it."

"So be it," Smethurst said. "To be honest, I felt sorry for Oscar. I'd known him on and off for some time and he'd had some bad luck. His first wife died, you know, and it hit him very hard. They were a very close couple.

"He married again and I believe his second marriage broke up acrimoniously.

"Then there's that sister of his, Stella. A little of her goes a long way, I can tell you. Poor bloke."

Smethurst paused, tapping his fingers together. The detectives maintained their silence. The Smethursts didn't seem to be aware that Dover had died and it might be advantageous not to mention the fact until it was necessary to do so.

"We were downsizing," he finally said. "The children had left home and we didn't need that big rambling place any longer. We had quite a bit of stuff to get rid of. We didn't really need the money and, like I said, I felt sorry for Ossie so I gave him the chance to make an offer for anything of value.

"We sold him some of the stuff and he paid us out of his back pocket."

"He had wads of notes tucked away in those scruffy trousers," Mrs Smethurst commented. "I was quite shocked. I told him someone would kill him for it. He just laughed."

"And this was the only time you did business with him?" Swift asked.

"Yes and no," Smethurst said. "We sorted out the rest of the stuff we decided was surplus to our requirements and he came round and quickly made an offer for the lot. A bit too quickly. I noticed that he was particularly interested in a painting by a Lincolnshire artist we had hanging up in the hall, though he tried to disguise it. He made out that the painting and the artist were of little merit. So I told him I'd changed my mind and we'd keep the painting.

"He upped his offer for the job lot, including the painting, which he said he'd taken a bit of a fancy to for his own home despite its alleged lack of value. Having extracted a little more blood out of the stone, and because we wanted to get rid quickly, I agreed and we arranged for him to come round with a van the next week.

"A day later he rang to say he could only get use of the van that Sunday and seeing that we wanted to get the house clear he made it sound as if he was doing us a favour. Big mistake.

"We had been watching Antiques Road Show on the telly before he turned up. It was being broadcast from Lincoln and, lo and behold, someone had brought along a picture by the same artist. According to the expert, it was well known among dealers that this artist was in fashion and prices for his work were rising.

"So when Ossie turned up I told him the deal was off."

"And how did he take it?" Swift asked.

"Badly," Mrs Smethurst butted in with real venom. "I won't

repeat what he called Charlie, especially not in front of two polite young ladies. He threatened us both. He scared me."

"He tried to make out we had a contract," her husband said more calmly. "Of course, we hadn't. There was nothing in writing. He knew perfectly well a handshake wouldn't stand up in a court of law. He was all talk."

Mrs Smethurst was getting positively agitated.

"No he wasn't," she insisted. "He has friends. Nasty men. He said he'd send them round and he did."

"Please keep calm dear," Mr Smethurst said. "This isn't doing your blood pressure any good."

"Then you tell him," his wife said in anguish, her face turning brighter red.

Swift started to get alarmed. The last thing she wanted to do was spark a medical emergency, especially when it would lead to questions over what she and Smith were doing there in the first place.

"All right, all right," Mr Smethurst said. "Two men with balaclavas over their face and baseball bats in their hands called on us the next day. They told us Ossie Dover would be back later that week and we'd better have all the stuff ready for him to take."

"And did you get the stuff ready?" Swift asked.

"I hadn't much choice. Jessie here begged me to let him have everything he wanted and I was worried the strain would kill her. So yes, I got the stuff ready. But he never showed up for it. Like I said, he was all talk."

"You went to find him, didn't you?" Jessie Smethurst said.

"To find out why he didn't turn up, I assume," Swift asked.

Mr Smethurst nodded vigorously as she spoke.

"Yes," he said quickly. "But I couldn't find him, not at his shop or at the café where he used to sit out in all weathers. So I came home. We're still waiting. The stuff's piled up in the spare bedroom if you want to see it."

"No, dear," his wife persisted to Charlie Smethurst's visible annoyance. "I mean the day after those nasty men came. That was when you went to find him and couldn't."

The eyes of the two detectives turned expectantly on her

husband, who shifty uneasily in his seat.

"Oh yes," he said flustered. "I'd forgotten about that. I was going to find him but I got sidetracked by something else and didn't actually make it into Alford that day. I didn't like to tell you at the time," he added, shooting a dark look at his wife, "because I know how upset you were about the whole thing. Anyway, it didn't matter seeing as he never came back anyway."

"He didn't come back," Swift finally admitted, "because he died. Didn't you know?"

Both the Smethursts denied any knowledge of his death, the woman convincingly, the man rather less so.

The two police officers set off on the long walk back to their car, the possibility of afternoon tea at the windmill forgotten.

"We might as well just have a quick word with Janet Templeton, the owner of the café in the market square," Swift said. "If Charlie Smethurst knew that Oscar Dover sat drinking tea at the café it's likely that Templeton saw them together."

"It's worth a shot," Smith agreed.

They found Templeton alone at the café. Swift got straight to the point in case they were interrupted by the arrival of a customer.

"We've just been having a chat with Charlie Smethurst," Swift said. She realised she could not be certain that Templeton knew him.

"Uhuh," Templeton said absentmindedly.

Swift took that as confirmation that she did indeed know who Smethurst was.

"Was he here with Oscar Dover in the days just before Mr Dover died?"

Now she had Templeton's full attention.

"Did he say he was?" she asked.

"Does it make any difference to the answer?" Swift responded. She immediately regretted not lying and saying yes to put pressure on the café owner.

"I don't think so," Templeton said after a short hesitation. "I don't think so."

She sounded decidedly unconvincing.

Chapter 13

It was a week after the discovery that barium hydroxide had been stolen from a school attended by Oscar Dover's children. Detective Inspector Paul Amos was feeling bored out of his skull.

Administration did not come easy to him, although mercifully the Chief Constable's assistant David handled that side of the operation brilliantly. What was really frustrating was organising other people to go out and do the job in hand while he was stuck at headquarters.

Not that Amos actually wanted to go out to the schools himself under Sir Robert Fletcher's latest pet project but he hated ordering other officers to do anything that he was not prepared to do himself. Once the project was rolling it was not proving to be a full time job for both him and David.

Unfortunately, this project was lasting longer than most of Sir Robert's flights of fancy and the favourable publicity that it continued to generate in Lincolnshire newspapers, along with multiple letters from readers supporting the scheme, simply stoked the Chief Constable's enthusiasm.

Finally, Amos announced to David that he felt he really should visit a second school "just to make sure that the project remained on track".

David at first seemed very unsure. How things had changed. At the start the Chief Constable's private secretary would have been only too pleased to get a break from sharing an office with Amos, whom he still openly distrusted despite his relief that the inspector had not provided any cause for Fletcher to have a fit of pique.

However, after mysteriously disappearing for a few minutes David re-emerged to declare that "I've been thinking about it and it seems a great idea for you to demonstrate real leadership."

Amos's appearance at a school, according to David's sudden

conversion to the idea, would show the troops that "the senior officers were firmly behind them and it would underline the folly of those who had found excuses not to take part or who had done so grudgingly".

He added enthusiastically: "I'm sure Sir Robert will thoroughly approve of you leading from the front."

Of course you're sure, Amos thought. You've just asked him. You wouldn't have dared to be so condescending towards me if you hadn't.

However, he pretended not to realise that David had obviously run it past the Chief Constable in order to cover his own back. David quickly looked at the schedule on his desk.

"You could take Spilsby tomorrow morning," he said.

Amos agreed immediately. Spilsby was 30 miles to the east of police headquarters. The further away the local officers were based from the Chief Constable, the more openly hostile they were to the project, so it was difficult to find local officers to fill the speaking slots.

Besides, Amos could drag out the visit, driving there and back in leisurely fashion and perhaps even have a bite of lunch sitting in the sunshine at an outdoor cafe if the weather held up.

David passed Amos briefing notes on the school in question. The small market town had originally had a grammar school, named after its founder King Edward VI, and a secondary modern, the Franklin, commemorating the arctic explorer who was born locally. These had now been amalgamated on the Franklin site just outside the town centre.

Maintaining a sixth form with comparatively few student staying on at the grammar school had proved impracticable so pupils at the amalgamated school were aged only up to 16.

It did occur to Amos that the more ambitious pupils would travel to Skegness, Alford or Horncastle where they could continue through to A levels and he would possibly be left to face an unruly group of teenagers. In the event he was heard politely by a genuinely interested set of 15 and 16-year-olds.

It was actually a member of staff who was harder to control. One female teacher insisted on posing a wide range of questions, several times asking effectively the same question but in a different form of words. She encouraged the pupils to engage more keenly and supplied addendums to their queries.

Such was the rapport that Amos managed to build that it was just after noon when he emerged into the school car park and drove into Spilsby market square. He didn't really mind too much. It delayed his reluctant return to the pleasure of David's company.

He selected a cafe opposite the statue of Spilsby's famous son, Sir John Franklin, ordered an all-day breakfast at the counter, opting for fried tomato rather than baked beans as it sounded more healthy, and chose a table nearest the road, since this would retain the sunshine for longer as the sun moved westwards.

The café was almost empty but it took a quite a few minutes for his meal to arrive. Amos wished he had had the foresight to buy a newspaper to read while he ate and was tempted to nip across to the newsagents he could see on the far side of Market Street when a young lady appeared with a full plate.

Amos was more hungry than he expected and was halfway through his meal when a car came along the High Street. The street was one-way to traffic, widening slightly into two lanes as it swung into Market Street.

The car came round a little too quickly, veered over to the right lane then swung back sharply to the left with a screech of tyres. The driver hesitated at the junction to allow a lorry to come past then pulled out impatiently behind it.

The driver was past Amos in a blur but the inspector vaguely recognised the shape of the man, though he couldn't think where from.

A few moments later he remembered. The driver had parked and was walking towards him purposefully. It was the science master Tim Armstrong from the school at Alford.

The teacher took a seat, saying: "Do you mind if I join you?"

"Looks like you just did," Amos replied dryly. He hated eating while someone who was not eating sat and watched.

Armstrong fidgeted nervously, apparently struggling for what to say.

"Don't tell me this is a coincidence," Amos said caustically. "You obviously came to say something. Spit it out."

Amos's irritability unsettled Armstrong further. He looked away, giving Amos the opportunity to consume a forkful of food without having to do so under the teacher's gaze.

"Let me guess. One of the teachers at Spilsby tipped you off that I was there. Probably the one who tried to spin out the session to give you time to get here."

The man seated opposite him nodded.

"She knew I'd been worried sick about this business of the barium hydroxide going missing from the lab," he said. "This could cost me my career. I got to the school as fast as I could but you'd already left. I wouldn't have seen you if I hadn't gone for a sandwich."

Then the teacher added urgently: "I need to know. Are you going to take it any further?"

"Does the headmaster know you are playing truant?" Amos asked casually.

"He knows I'm here," Armstrong said sharply. "Look, none of us want any trouble."

Amos decided not to say that he had, in fact, rather forgotten about the incident. He had enough on his mind treading warily through the Chief Constable's schools project while checking surreptitiously that Det Sgt Juliet Swift was managing fine without him.

Besides, the incident was some time ago and if, as Amos suspected, the school would close ranks and try to deny that anything untoward had happened it was probably more trouble than it was worth to pursue the matter. The Chief Constable might feel that other schools would be reluctant to take part in the project if they feared that some past indiscretion conveniently buried would come to light when the police came snooping round.

"I haven't done anything about it," Amos said simply.

"That's not what I asked you," the teacher said with new-found aggression. "I assumed you hadn't done anything yet or I would have heard about it pretty smartish. The question is whether you are planning to take the matter further."

"Probably not," Amos said after a pause. He stared the teacher straight in the eye and added: "As long as it doesn't have any bearing on any crime committed, you're in the clear. But I can't guarantee it absolutely."

"Well, if anyone cops for this, I'm taking other people down with me. I don't see why I should get all the blame. You don't know how tough it is these days keeping kids under control. You try to impose discipline and the parents are down on you like a ton of bricks.

"You can't blame us for trying to hush things up."

"And what else has been hushed up?" Amos asked curiously. "You'd better tell me or I may think again about the raid on your store cupboard."

The threat was apparently superfluous, for Armstrong seemed to relish the opportunity to steer attention away from himself and onto his colleagues.

"Paedophiles," he said abruptly. "Paedophiles. We had young men hanging round the school gates at going home time. They were chatting to the sixth form girls. The head was wishy-washy about it as usual. I tried to warn the girls because the men were 10 or 20 years older than them but they just hitched up their skirts a couple of inches and lapped up the attention.

"I went to warn Oscar Dover about his daughter Julia. At least he was concerned. He said he would do something about it. As it happened, he didn't need to because a day or two later the men disappeared. Even so, I argued strenuously that we should call in the police. The head said it would ruin the good name of the school."

"Why Oscar Dover?" Amos asked, his curiosity aroused. "Did you get to see any of the other parents?"

Armstrong was clearly flustered.

"Well I ... er ... well I just thought Julia was the most vulnerable," he finally managed to gabble unconvincingly. "Anyway, what has that got to do with anything?"

Amos merely raised his eyebrows.

"All right, then, do your worst," he suddenly said petulantly.

With that, Armstrong stormed off to his parked car.

Chapter 14

Amos abandoned his half eaten breakfast, which was now tepid despite enjoying the rays of the sun, ambled into the café to pay at the counter then retrieved his own car from the High Street.

Why was it, he wondered, OK to park for an hour for free where cars hampered the movement of buses in the narrow road, but you had to pay if you did the decent thing and put your vehicle onto the parking bays in the market square?

Not my problem, he thought. I've got enough of my own trying to run this education programme with David.

Despite his desire to spin out the visit to Spilsby for as long as possible, he wanted to get back to Lincoln to discuss with DS Swift his encounter at the café.

He had planned to take the most direct route back, though Hundleby and Lusby to join the main Lincoln Road at Scrafield Fork, stopping en route at the vantage point where, on a fine day like this, you could see Boston Stump, Tattershall Castle and Lincoln Cathedral in the distance.

The stop for the scenic view would have to be ditched. He could, without taking risks, get back to headquarters by 1.30pm, when David, a late lunchtaker, would be in the canteen and would not spot him slipping into CID on his way back to the top floor office they shared.

Amos and Swift tended to start work an hour before David and therefore to get hungry correspondingly earlier. There was a fair chance Swift would be in CID when Amos got back – and so it proved.

Even better, Jennifer, the civilian assistant whom Amos suspected of reporting back to the Chief Constable, albeit on a lesser scale than David, was absent.

The inspector gave a casual, almost imperceptible flick of his head as he walked through to his office. Swift took the hint and followed.

"Are you still working on the Oscar Dover case?" Amos asked as soon as Swift had closed the door behind her.

"Yes and no," she said with a sigh. "I'm still keeping an open mind but there's nothing much more to go on. I've been filling in the time with a few burglaries round Scampton. The male officers lost interest when they found it had nothing to do with the RAF station. Lawnmovers and wheelbarrows don't compete with the Red Arrows."

"I've just had an interesting conversation with Armstrong, the chemistry teacher," Amos said. "For a start, he's panic stricken over the stealing of some chemical, whatever it was, from his lab. But that wasn't what I wanted to tell you about. As a sop, he tried to buy me off by raising an alternative issue.

"He told me that men aged up to 40 years old used to hang round the school chatting up the senior girls as they left."

"So what's new?"

"He described them as paedophiles, which at first I thought was a bit over the top. But he felt sufficiently strongly about it to go round to warn Julia Dover's father to watch out for his daughter."

"I'm still not sure where this takes us," Swift said.

"First of all, I wonder why Tim Armstrong was so concerned about Julia in particular." Amos said. "I think he was after her for himself. I doubt if that would go down well with our friend Oscar. Could the two of them have clashed?"

Swift looked doubtful.

"I can't think that's enough to merit reopening the case," she said.

"No, I agree. But there was something more that I found quite curious," Amos went on. "The day after Armstrong went to speak to Oscar Dover, the men disappeared. I don't think Armstrong thought it was anything more than a coincidence but it struck me that the two events were connected. Armstrong sees Oscar Dover and Dover tells the men to back off. I'm not a great believer in coincidences."

"But I just don't see how such a poor specimen of a man as Oscar Dover could see off a bunch of youths."

"It's amazing what a parent can do when they see their

children in danger," Amos pointed out, "but no, I really can't see that happening. And even if Dover turned up and turned nasty, why didn't the young men just drift back a few days later? Dover couldn't park himself outside the school at leaving time every day, surely.

"Armstrong called them paedophiles. Were they part of a group of which Dover was a member? It sounds a bit far fetched but that's the only reason I can think of that rings true. Dover was something of an oddball, leading an increasingly lonely life and becoming estranged from his family. Did he have a darker side? Much darker than just being in possession of dirty photographs, bad as that is.

"We know there's a paedophile ring operating along the east coast but so far neither us nor Norfolk police have been able to get anywhere near it. It would be a great feather in your cap if you cracked it."

"So the question is whether I waste any more time in the hope of rescuing something from this mess," Swift said. "Not so much throwing good money after bad as throwing good time after bad."

"It's up to you," Amos said. "You're your own boss at the moment. I have to get back to the grindstone."

He left Swift to ponder. She broke her rule of avoiding speaking to Jennifer and borrowed the map of Lincolnshire that the CID officer manager kept on her shelf, the one that was treasured because it showed most of the county in sufficient detail without the road you wanted disappearing off the edge of the page and into the next map.

The garden shed raiders had spread their attention eastwards to around the villages of Welton, where they had unsuccessfully tried to break into the golf club offices, and Dunholme to the north east of police HQ at Nettleham. It would be easy from there to slip onto the A46 Market Rasen road and then cut eastwards to Louth.

She'd probably have time on her hands after making a cursory check of the properties involved and there would be little chance of finding any real clues as to the perpetrators. There was nothing to go home for. Her long-term boyfriend was still returning home late on the pretext that he was working overtime, though Swift didn't believe him.

If she finished early on the burglaries, she would go to see the two daughters of Oscar Dover. If not she would go home.

Fate tossed the hypothetical coin and it came down early. Swift drove to Louth. Fate also decreed that both sisters were at home when she arrived.

Lynn answered the door and let the detective sergeant in without hesitation; as soon as Julia saw who the visitor was, she blurted out to her sister: "What did you let her in for?"

Lynn sat down sullenly while Julia continued to glare. Swift ignored them and sat down.

"The men who used to hang round your school gates," she said peremptorily.

"What about them?" Julia demanded.

"Did they bother you?" Swift asked.

"Not particularly," Julia replied.

"And how about you?"

This time the question was directed at Lynn.

The younger sister shifted uneasily.

"Not particularly," she said unconvincingly.

"And did they bother your father?"

"Not particularly," Julia butted in. "Why would they? He wasn't gay."

"He had two teenage daughters running the gauntlet of these lads. I think that might bother any parent," Swift said tartly. "Did either of you go out with any of them?"

Julia merely raised her eyes to the ceiling with a look of scorn. Lynn again shifted uneasily.

"Did your father go and warn them off?" Swift persisted.

"Don't be ridiculous," Julia said with contempt. "They'd have beaten him to a pulp."

"And yet, the day after one of your teachers came to warn him about them, they disappeared."

Now it was Julia's turn to look uncomfortable, although both girls remained silent.

Seeing she was getting nowhere, Swift tried a new tack. What she lacked in Amos's diplomacy she made up for in forthrightness. Sometimes shock tactics paid off.

"Did your father ever interfere with you?" she asked.

Both girls gasped audibly.

"He most certainly did not," Julia almost shouted. "How dare you?"

Lynn remained strangely silent.

"Tell her he didn't, Lynn," Julia was almost screaming now. "Tell the bitch."

Lynn, however, merely nodded and burst into tears.

"I'm not here to judge you," Swift said gently.

She couldn't think what else to say. She wasn't quite sure how she had expected the interview to go but it definitely wasn't like this.

"It was horrible," Lynn sobbed. "Thank goodness it's all over."

"You shouldn't have told her about it," Julia said without the slightest hint of empathy. "It's none of her business. You should have said no like I told you."

"Don't tell me what I should and shouldn't do," Lynn snapped back. "Where were you when I needed your help. You abandoned me to him. You could have done something."

"I didn't know," Julia retorted.

"That's because you were too wrapped up with Mr Armstrong to pay any attention to me."

"I was not," Julia said indignantly. The two girls were talking across Swift as if she wasn't there. "Don't you dare try to put the blame on Tim just because of what Dad did. It was after Tim came that Dad stopped, wasn't it?"

"I thought you said you didn't know," Lynn screamed. "Well I'm not sorry now that Dad beat up your precious Tim. It serves you right."

With that riposte, Lynn stormed out of the room and stamped up the stairs.

Swift felt rising anger at the thought of a father abusing his own daughter. However, Oscar Dover was now beyond the reach of the law. Instead, she turned back to Julia.

"You'd better tell me about you and Tim Armstrong," Swift said sternly as the noise of Lynn's departure abated. "Your teacher had a duty of care towards you and it's a serious matter if he took advantage of a pupil."

"Nothing happened, honest," Julia protested. "Lynn was making it all up. Tim … I mean Mr Armstrong came round here out of genuine concern. Dad got the wrong end of the stick and started hitting him but Mr Armstrong backed off. He could have easily taken on Dad but he did the decent thing and walked away. It's not fair pointing the finger at him."

"Did Mr Armstrong warn the other parents of girls in your year?"

"He was going to but, like you said, the men disappeared so there was no need."

"Did you steal the barium hydroxide?"

"No, I did not."

"Do you know who did, and what happened to it?"

"Yes, but I'm not saying. You can't make me. I don't tell tales."

Suddenly Swift and Julia were aware that Lynn was standing in the doorway, her face like thunder.

"She flushed it down the toilet," Lynn said. "At least, that's what she made out. She didn't want precious Tim getting into trouble."

Julia rose to her feet.

"That's quite enough," she said angrily.

"Did she tell you about the slushy letter he sent her, pledging his undying love?" Lynn said to Swift, ignoring her sister.

"I told you, that's quite enough," Julia repeated even more angrily. "Did you tell Dad?"

"I traded the information in return for being left alone," Lynn said. "You didn't help me so why shouldn't I land you in it? He wasn't best pleased when he saw the letter."

Julia sat down again, the blood visibly draining from her face.

"He couldn't have seen the letter," she protested unconvincingly. "I never let it out of my sight."

"It seems you did," Lynn said triumphantly, her mood transformed. "You left it in your desk. Maria Dawson found it and made copies. She sold them for 50p each. There were plenty of takers. Would you believe some of your classmates were actually jealous?"

Julia fell into a shocked silence, which only encouraged her sister to turn the screw. Lynn, who had, unnoticed by the other two, kept her right arm down by her side with the hand tucked slightly behind her back, turned to Swift and produced a piece of paper with a flourish.

"Would you like to read it?" she asked the detective, holding the paper out to her.

Julia leapt up to grab it but Swift reacted more quickly, taking the paper and turning her back on the elder sister to keep it out of her reach.

"It's mine," Julia demanded. "Hand it to me."

"No it's not," Lynn retorted triumphantly. "It belongs to me. I paid 50p for it."

Swift looked at the contentious document. It was a photostat of a letter written in a careful, legible hand. There were no crossings out or insertions. The writer had presumably thought through what he wanted to say.

A quick glance told Swift that the letter was addressed to "my dearest, darling Julia". One paragraph promised that "it won't be long before we can be together all the time, my darling".

Apparently the writer thought that Julia "was mature beyond her years" but she had to be patient because "we cannot consummate our beautiful love while you are still at school".

It was impossible for Swift to read more than odd snatches – although that was still enough to get the general drift of the missive – because Julia was jostling round her trying unsuccessfully to snatch the precious letter.

So Swift folded it up and put it into an inside pocket in her jacket.

Seeing that protestations were pointless, Julia sat down, allowing Swift, who kept a wary distance with the sofa as a buffer between them, to take the document out again and continue reading, glancing every few seconds in case Julia made another grab for the letter.

Concentrate on your A levels, Julia was urged, although "I

know how hard it is to concentrate when you are thinking about me because I find it so hard to concentrate on my lessons when all my waking thoughts as well as my dreams are all about you".

The letter continued: "When the A levels are over we will make beautiful, passionate love all night for ever more."

There were various protestations of love that would have made Venus herself blush and an assurance that "just because I resist temptation it doesn't mean I don't love you – I am thinking about what is best for both of us".

Swift refolded the photostat and put it safely back into her pocket.

"You're not keeping it," Julia protested.

"I certainly am," Swift replied. "You've just opened up a new line of inquiry."

Chapter 15

Swift could hear the two sisters arguing volubly as she left the house. Now she was in the area, she wanted to try to catch Tim Armstrong at home to get his version of events but she didn't have his address and she didn't fancy facing the girls again.

In any case, even if she did go back, there was no reason to assume that they would have their teacher's address. Swift had never had more than a faint idea where any of her own teachers had lived.

A glance at the letter did no more than confirm what Swift already knew. There was no address at the top of it.

Julia probably did not visit Armstrong at his home if, as the letter implied, they had not consummated their beautiful love and she would probably not willingly give Swift the address, even if she had it. She was more likely to have her besotted teacher's phone number, in which case she could alert him before Swift could get to him.

The detective sergeant decided to take pot luck and drive to the school. The place was not quite in darkness. A caretaker was busy cleaning up in one of the classrooms. He nearly jumped out of his skin when Swift tapped on the window.

Lights now came on down a corridor as the caretaker made his way to the front door.

"Sorry to give you a fright," Swift said pleasantly as the caretaker opened the door on sight of her warrant card through the glass. "A bit of a long shot but I need to get in touch with a member of the teaching staff urgently. Do you have a list of addresses?"

"One of the kids in trouble again?" the caretaker asked. "Don't tell me. I don't want to know. None of my business."

He opened the door wider and waved Swift inside.

"You're quite right," Swift said. "You really don't want to know."

"If you come through to the office there's a list there. Any particular teacher in mind or will any one do?"

The caretaker unlocked the office, turned on the lights and produced a list from the top drawer of a desk. There was no need to go into detail.

"This one will do," Swift said pointing at Armstrong's name as if she had picked it at random. "Is this address anywhere near here?"

"I don't know," the caretaker said. "There's a map on the wall."

Swift studied the map and located the road where Armstrong lived.

"Yes," she said as if making a decision. "This one will do."

"Do you want me to ring him to make sure he's in?" the caretaker asked.

"I'm sure he will be," Swift said. "He'll probably be marking homework. Thanks a lot for your help."

Swift carefully memorised the relatively simple route to Armstrong's address from the map and departed purposefully. The caretaker locked the door behind her as she left.

Armstrong was indeed at home, though with a glass of scotch on the rocks in his hand rather than a school exercise book. This was evidently a night off from marking homework.

The relaxed look on Armstrong's face, induced presumably by the liquid in his glass, vanished as Swift produced her warrant card.

"You'd better come in," he said resignedly. "I suppose this is about the missing chemical. It was no big deal but if you're going to pursue this just tell me and I'll quit my job. It'll be the end of my career but there it is."

"I'm not here about the chemical," she said smoothly as they entered the living room of Armstrong's home. "I'm here about Julia Dover."

"What about her?" Armstrong said cautiously. "She's left school. I don't know where she is."

"You're not married, I take it," Swift said, ignoring Armstrong's response.

"No. Does it matter?"

"It would matter to your wife if you were married and were carrying on with a sixth form girl."

"Well, I'm not married and I'm not carrying on with a sixth form girl," Armstrong said petulantly. "Nor have I ever done. Was there anything else?"

"You went round to see Julia Dover's father," Swift continued, again ignoring Armstrong's comments. "Tell me about that."

"I went to see Julia's father because there were men hanging around the school gates," Armstrong said steadily and deliberately. "We complained to the police about it but they said there was nothing they could do because it was a public highway.

"I thought the parents ought to know, especially those with sixth form girls at the school. Did you think I went to ask for his daughter's hand in marriage?"

"Yet I understand that your concern stretched only to Julia Dover. I understand you didn't call on any of the other parents. Why was that?"

"You seem to understand quite a lot," Armstrong said, patently rattled. "Anyway, there was no need. The men disappeared so there was nothing more that needed doing."

"I understand," Swift said provocatively, "I understand Mr Dover wasn't particularly grateful for your concern."

"Well, you understand wrong."

"I don't think so. I think Julia's father had seen the letter."

"What letter?" Armstrong protested without conviction. He looked visibly alarmed but also shocked.

Swift looked at him carefully.

"You didn't know, did you?" she said. "You didn't know that the letter had been copied?"

Armstrong slumped back into his seat and shook his head.

"Apparently one of the girls in Julia's class spotted the letter in her desk," Swift explained. "She borrowed it and photostatted it before putting it back. She sold copies at 50p each and I've been told there was no shortage of takers."

"How do you know?"

"I've seen a copy of the letter. I don't think Julia knew it had been copied until today."

"We didn't have sex," Armstrong blurted out. "I didn't do anything wrong."

"I believe you," Swift said, "about the sex, that is. But you still crossed the line in your relationship with a pupil. More to the point, Julia's father didn't believe you, did he?"

Armstrong shook his head again.

"I'm afraid he made his views very plain. He kept hitting me and I couldn't hit back for fear of offending Julia. I had to keep backing away and once I was out of the door make a dash for it."

"And instead of being grateful, Julia thought you were a coward and dropped you."

This time Armstrong nodded.

"So you were pretty angry with Mr Dover," Swift pressed. "He beats you up, he stops you seeing Julia and Julia drops you. That's a pretty lousy way of repaying your concern for his daughter."

"Yes," Armstrong said simply. "Look, are you taking this business between me and Julia further? I'm getting tired of being played along. Where do I stand?"

"It depends how helpful you are. Did you go back to see Mr Dover again? You knew where to find him."

"No."

"You sure?"

"Of course I'm sure. I know whether I saw him or not. I didn't want to get beaten up again. I kept well clear."

Perhaps Julia was right, Swift thought. Perhaps he really is a coward. There was a second reason why she wanted to talk to Armstrong.

"Anyway," Swift went on pleasantly, "There's something that interests me more than your grubby little dalliance. Did you know any of the men outside the school?

"If I give you a name, will you get off my back?" Armstrong asked anxiously.

"No promises," Swift replied, "but if I go off in search of the men I might just forget about you."

"I recognised one of them," Armstrong said. "He used to

attend the school. He was the youngest one in the group so he stuck out a bit. I'll write down his name and address."

Chapter 16

Sensing his opportunity to get rid of Swift, hopefully for good, Armstrong gave her copious instructions how to cover the short distance to the home of Kevin Shoesmith, the name on the piece of paper.

By Armstrong's calculations, Shoesmith would now be in his late 20s but was, the chemistry teacher believed, still living at home.

A substantial home it was, too, as Swift realised when she pulled up outside the detached house in a tree-lined street. A security light came on as she approached the front door.

Swift pressed the bell and could hear Westminster chimes ringing in the interior. A few seconds later a burly man in his fifties, a good six foot tall, answered the door and looked aggressively at the unexpected visitor on his doorstep.

He was distinctly unimpressed when Swift showed her warrant card and distinctly displeased when she asked to speak to Kevin Shoesmith.

"What's he done now?" the man demanded. "Just tell me and I'll deal with it. It won't happen again, whatever he's done."

"Is Kevin at home?" Swift demanded unperturbed. "I'd like to speak to him."

"What's it about?"

"I'll tell Kevin. I believe he is an adult."

After a few moments of stand-off on the doorstep, the man who Swift took, correctly as it turned out, to be Kevin Shoesmith's father reluctantly allowed the officer access to the house.

"Come here Kevin and get this sorted," Shoesmith bellowed up the stairs as he led Swift into the living room.

"Take a seat," he added ungraciously to Swift. She did as she was bid, deciding that the question of whether to sit or stand was not an issue to fight over.

Kevin could be heard almost falling down the stairs in his haste to answer his father's summons.

"This lady detective wants a word with you," Shoesmith senior said, fingering the metal buckle of the broad belt he wore round his trousers. "Your explanation had better be good. Well sit down," he added roughly. His belt buckle snapped open with an audible click.

Kevin made no attempt to ascertain what he was supposed to have done wrong. He glanced anxiously at Swift, who could see that he was struggling to control his shaking. His father stood there glowering.

"I think it would be better if we talked in private," Swift said coldly and firmly.

After a moment's hesitation, Shoesmith senior left the room, but not before launching a parting shot: "You'd better tell her the truth."

"The truth about what?" Swift asked innocently the moment she and Kevin were left alone. It did no harm to let Kevin Shoesmith guess at why she was there and perhaps tell her something she was not aware of.

"I don't know," Kevin stammered almost in tears. "I don't know what I'm supposed to have done, honestly."

This is a grown man acting like a six-year-old, Swift thought in astonishment. Why on earth doesn't he leave home?

She decided, given his fragile state, not to push him too hard, however.

"It's about the company you keep, Kevin," she said gently. "Or at least, did keep. The men who used to hang about outside schools harassing teenage girls."

At this point Shoesmith senior burst back into the room in dramatic fashion. It had not occurred to Swift, who cursed herself for the oversight, that he would be listening outside. He must have had his ear against the door to hear her, as she had spoken quietly.

"What's this about?" he demanded furiously to his son, pulling his now unfastened belt one way and then the other through the loops of his trousers.

Visibly shaking, the younger Shoesmith blurted out: "I

didn't go near the girls. It was Barry Wright. He was the one. I didn't do anything."

Shoesmith senior's anger subsided remarkably quickly, although he was by now winding the belt round his knuckles.

"Kevin fell in with a bad lot," he explained to Swift. "This Barry Wright was no good. He's a lot older than Kevin. He's been in prison twice already. I stopped Kevin from having anything to do with them when I found out who he was knocking about with and you've never been in trouble have you, Kevin? I know my duties as a parent and I take them seriously."

I bet you do, Swift thought. She decided it was pointless to ask Shoesmith to let her question Kevin alone. Although the young man was no longer a child he was still vulnerable and it was probably best to interview him in the presence of a responsible adult, though preferably not his father, if a formal interview at a police station proved to be necessary.

"Did any of you approach the girls outside the school?" Swift asked Kevin. "I mean actually go up to them and engage them in conversation."

"I didn't," he replied nervously, "but one or two of the others did – the ones who'd already been out with girls or pretended they had. But they didn't do anything they shouldn't have. They just talked to them."

"Were the girls frightened?"

"I don't think so."

"Did Barry Wright or anyone else in the group ever touch any of the girls, to the best of your knowledge?"

"Barry did one time. He and one of the girls went off with their arms round each other. They were snogging. She didn't seem to mind. He didn't use force."

"Do you know who the girl was?"

"No, I didn't know her myself. Barry called her Julia."

"How long did this go on?"

"Only a few days."

"Did any of the teachers try to stop you?" Swift sought confirmation of what Armstrong had told her.

"One did," Kevin replied. "This Julia girl said it was the

chemistry teacher. She just laughed when he tried to threaten Barry with the police."

"Did anyone else intervene?"

"The day after the chemistry teacher, we were hanging round the school gates waiting for the girls to come out when this weird old bloke came storming up and gave Barry a real mouthful. We thought Barry would make mincemeat of him but you could tell the old man frightened him.

"I'd never seen Barry scared before. He tried to laugh it off and told us to come along as he walked away but we could all tell he was really scared. The gang broke up after that. Barry was supposed to be the leader and he was scared of an old man."

"Did you hear what the old man said?" Swift asked.

Kevin Shoesmith shook his head.

"Barry backed away from him as soon as he showed up so he was a bit away from the rest of us," he answered. "The man had his back to us and he spoke very quietly so none of us except Barry heard what he said. Afterwards none of us felt like asking Barry what on earth had happened. We didn't want to humiliate him further."

"Just one more question," Swift said. "Did Barry ever show you any dirty photographs?"

Kevin glanced nervously at his father before replying in a barely audible voice: "Yes. He used to show them to us. They were really disgusting."

"Did you recognise anyone on the pictures."

"No – but I didn't look at them properly," Kevin added quickly. "No-one else said they recognised anyone and I'm sure they would have said."

"Is that the truth?" Shoesmith senior demanded menacingly, flexing his belt. "It had better be."

"Yes honest, Dad," Kevin stammered.

"I believe you," Swift assured them both. "Everything you said fits in with what I already know."

Shoesmith senior relaxed noticeably and started to thread his belt back through the loops on the waistband of his trousers.

"He doesn't have the guts to break the law," he said. "The

trouble with Kevin is he's a mamby pamby. A mummy's boy. His mother babied him. I should have put my foot down."

Swift saw no point in trying to take up the cudgels on his son's behalf. She very much doubted that he had failed to invoke discipline but there was little point in saying so. However, Shoesmith senior took the lack of contradiction as confirmation that Kevin did indeed need to man up.

"He's never held down a proper job," the father continued with relish. "No use on a farm, no use in a factory. Doesn't like to get his hands dirty. His trouble is he's had too much time on his hands. He's always locking himself away in that shed in the back garden painting pictures that no one in their right minds would want to buy."

Kevin had risen to his feet when he thought Swift had finished the interrogation and was now shrinking back against the wall. Like the well-honed bully that he was, his father was encouraged by fear in his victim.

"Show her the pictures," he demanded, stretching out his arm towards Kevin with his palm upwards. "Come on, hand over the key.

"He's the only person who's got a key," Shoesmith added to Swift. "We used to have two and I think he lost the other one on purpose to stop us seeing what he gets up to locked in there on his own."

"Please Dad," his son pleaded. "I'm sure she doesn't want to see."

Unfortunately for the young man, Swift's curiosity was aroused by his obvious reluctance to comply. Why was the budding artist so reluctant for anyone to see what was in the shed? She wondered if the refuge in the back garden would offer any insights into the case.

Shoesmith senior glared silently and menacingly, one hand remaining outstretched and the other fingering his belt buckle. His son reluctantly produced a heavy mortice key from his pocket. His father snatched it from his hand and hurried off to the back door, Swift following smartly and Kevin sullenly.

The back garden was mainly a mess of brambles and nettles competing for space. Kevin certainly didn't dirty his hands on it, nor did anyone else. Blackberry flowers were dotted all over the brambles and the ones with greatest access to the sun were already turning to berries.

The only exception to the mass of hostile foliage was a well-trodden path to a large shed that had seen better days. Shoesmith senior turned the key on the lock and flung open the door, the draught disturbing paintings scattered on the floor and a bench. Others pinned to the wall fluttered momentarily.

Swift was the only one of the three who actually stepped inside.

If she was hoping to uncover pornography, she was doomed to disappointment. As she looked round the paintings she quickly realised that not one contained a single human being, naked or otherwise.

They depicted unrelieved gloom, with dark threatening skies and blackened buildings. Most of the edifices were clearly recognisable as Lincoln landmarks, though not as Swift knew them.

Roads turned off at odd angles, leaving the buildings squashed into uncomfortably shaped plots. The roads and alleyways all narrowed into dead ends. Lincoln's magnificent cathedral was transformed into a grotesque structure shortened to half its real length with the twin towers above the West door splayed out as if about to crash to the ground.

The contents of the shed conveyed a massive cry for help that Swift felt unable to provide. She came back out into the garden, closed the door gently and led the way back to the house.

As she did so she asked casually: "Is this Barry Wright still around? I take it he lives, or lived, locally."

Wright, like Kevin Shoesmith, had not left the area. He lived quite close by.

Unlike Shoesmith, however, he was decidedly uncooperative. When DS Swift turned up on his doorstep a few minutes after leaving the Shoesmiths, Barry Wright slammed the door in her face the moment she identified herself.

Time had moved on rather further than Swift had realised. Although she drove home rapidly with the sirens and blue flashing light on, she arrived to find her boyfriend Jason had already beaten her to it. There followed a blazing row over the long hours she was once again working.

Chapter 17

Two days later Amos was surprised to see Juliet Swift appear at the door of the office he now shared with the Chief Constable's dogsbody David. Amos never ventured onto the top floor of Lincolnshire police headquarters unless summoned, which happened mercifully rarely, and that attitude had rubbed off onto the detective sergeant.

Swift looked decidedly disconcerted. She hardly acknowledged David, giving him only with the most cursory of glances. David rarely liked to miss anything that could be reported back to Sir Robert Fletcher but such was Swift's obvious discomfort, and such was his reluctance to jeopardise his unexpectedly smooth working relationship with Amos, that he took the hint and made a feeble excuse to leave the room.

"What on earth is it?" Amos asked anxiously as soon as David was out of the door.

"You'd better see this," Swift said grimly, handing an envelope to Amos.

It had been slit open with a paperknife.

"You can pull the letter out," Swift said. "It's been checked for fingerprints and there aren't any apart from mine when I opened the envelope."

Amos extracted the single piece of paper. The message on it had been written in block capitals with a ball point pen. It read, somewhat melodramatically: "LET OSCAR DOVER REST IN PEACE. STOP POKING AROUND. YOU HAVE BEEN WARNED."

He tossed the sheet of paper onto the desk without commenting and examined the envelope, which had been posted with a first class stamp. It was addressed with the same block capitals and black ballpoint ink as the brief message it had carried. It was addressed to Swift at her home. The postmark was Doncaster with the previous day's date.

"Doesn't narrow it down much," Amos remarked drily. "All

the post from round here goes to Doncaster and back these days. Still, it's a reasonable assumption in light of your enquiries that it was posted in Lincolnshire."

Swift was rapidly recovering her composure.

"Have you reported this?" Amos asked.

Swift shook her head.

"They'll just take me off the case and give it to a bloke," she said with a touch of bitterness. "Or worse still, drop it altogether."

"Have you honestly got anywhere with Oscar Dover's supposed murder?"

Another head shake from Swift.

"Not the murder, no," she said, "though there are plenty of grounds for thinking someone really did kill him. But this isn't about his death. It's about his life. And a pretty sordid one it degenerated into. I'm being warned off investigating a paedophile ring that he seems to have been a part of."

"Be careful, Juliet," Amos advised her. "These people have friends in high places. It's no disgrace to leave it alone. Do you have any actual evidence against anyone?"

Swift admitted that the chance of getting a conviction against anyone in the ring was even less than finding who, if anyone, killed Oscar Dover. What she did not admit to Amos was that she was now all the more determined to pursue her inquiries. While Amos was tied up with the Chief Constable's education initiative, there was nothing he could do to stop her.

Thus, later that day, Swift was back in the market place in Alford.

The café, as Swift had noted in her first visit, closed at 5pm, which seemed likely to be a good time to catch Janet Templeton alone again.

As it happened, two dawdlers were still finishing coffee and cake when she arrived at five minutes to five. Swift ordered a tea and immediately pulled out the money so there would be no misunderstanding this time over whether she would pay.

Templeton brought the beverage politely but with less than good grace.

"I'm sorry to rush you but we are about to close," she said

coldly.

The couple left and Templeton came to clear the table. To Swift's surprise, she noted that the café owner had slipped an engagement ring onto her finger, a ring that had not been there when Swift arrived, nor indeed on the detective sergeant's previous visit.

That matter could wait. Instead, she came straight to the point of her return: "Oscar Dover had photographs of you, didn't he?"

Templeton paused in mid-stride, visibly taken aback. After a few moments of silence she put the cups and plates down behind the counter and returned with an air or resignation.

"How did you find out?" she asked indignantly. "Stella promised me she would destroy them."

"Let's start at the beginning," Swift said, trying to hide her relief that not only had she surmised correctly but Templeton had not attempted to deny it.

Templeton was about to sit down when a tall, well-built man of similar age to her strode in through the door like the hero from a stereotypical romantic film, stepped the two or three paces between the tables, put his arm firmly but gently round her waist and plonked a kiss on her lips.

Seeing Templeton's lack of response, he pulled back without releasing her entirely and said in a concerned voice: "I'm sorry darling. Is something wrong?"

"Joe," the woman said urgently, "can you just leave us?"

Sensing his concern, she added hastily: "No, there's nothing wrong. And it's not you. This lady's a detective. She's just asking about someone I know."

"Do you want me to stay?" the man asked, his concern unassuaged.

"No, no," Templeton answered. "It's all right, really. Look," she added, taking a set of keys from her overall pocket and handing them to him, "wait for me at my flat. I'll be as quick as I can. And really, there is nothing to worry about."

The man looked doubtful but after a moment's hesitation did as he was asked.

No sooner was he out of the door than Templeton produced

another set of keys, locked up and turned the sign in the window from open to closed. She returned to Swift's table and sat down resignedly.

"Yes," she said simply, "as you apparently already know, Ossie Dover took photographs of me. It's hard to believe if you saw the shambling wreck he turned into but he was once a charming and charismatic young man. At first the pictures he took were entirely innocent and, frankly, I was flattered.

"Somehow he persuaded me to pose topless and then it seemed only a small step to fully nude. Afterwards I felt dirty. I was so ashamed and I begged him to give me the prints and the negatives but he refused point blank. The only consolation was that he promised that no-one else would ever see them and as far as I know he kept his word.

"I was just hoping his sister would do likewise, but apparently not."

Swift declined to put the woman out of her misery by admitting she had not, in fact, seen the photos. She was likely to learn more while Templeton was on edge.

Instead, Swift asked: "Did he attempt to blackmail you with them? Either for money or sexual favours."

Templeton shook her head.

"Mercifully I was spared that," she said. "I think he was actually genuinely fond of me in a warped sort of way.

"Except …" she paused. "It wasn't actually blackmail but one time he came to the café and sat outside with his back to the wall so no-one could come up behind him and after I'd taken him his tea he got out a package and opened it on the table.

"I didn't realise he had it until I popped back out unexpectedly. He'd got out some photographs. They were really disgusting. Far worse than the ones he'd taken of me. Some were of children. He scooped them up quickly when he saw me but it was too late. He stared right at me and said if I ever told anyone about it he'd show people the photos of me.

"I never said a word. I felt sorry for the children and I know I should have reported him but nothing I could have done altered the fact that the pictures had already been taken so I couldn't stop it.

"Anyway, I didn't think anyone would believe me. And I'm ashamed to say it gave me a bit of comfort. He knew that if he told any of my friends about the pictures of me I could get my revenge by reporting him to the police."

"I understand," Swift said with genuine sympathy. "You were in a very difficult position. You should have reported him, of course, but I can hardly blame you for wanting to get on with your life."

"Well, I tried to," Templeton said doubtfully. "Get on with my life, that is. But I never could commit to a man again – at least not until I met Joe. It's why I never married or even had a serious boyfriend. I was terrified any men who were interested in me – and there were one or two – would find out about my stupidity and naivety, even after Ossie himself was remarried and living in Louth.

"Then when he came to live with Stella I was at my wits end. I'd just taken up with Joe. He's wonderful and understanding. I was terrified Ossie would say something to him but he never did."

"Can you be sure?" Swift asked. "He might have told him without you knowing."

"Not a chance. Joe's the quietest, mildest man but if he'd found out about the photos Ossie Dover would have been a dead man walking. Joe would have beaten him to a pulp to protect me."

It seemed unlikely that Templeton was aware of Stella Dover's claim that someone had poisoned her brother. She clearly did not realise that she might be implicating her boyfriend. Templeton had a motive and also the opportunity, given that she was serving the alleged victim with frequent cups of tea; her boyfriend had a potential motive and, as he presumably came to the café, probably opportunity as well.

However, Swift wanted time to think things through, so she said: "I'm sure you're right. I can't be absolutely certain but I too doubt whether Oscar Dover said a word to Joe – or anyone else for that matter."

"Joe wanted to get engaged ages ago," Templeton continued,

"but I couldn't accept with the photos hanging over me. I wouldn't even agree to move in together and he's too much of a gentleman to press me to. But when Ossie died I felt able to accept his proposal of marriage.

"I still can't quite get used to the idea of wearing my engagement ring in case happiness is snatched from me after all. And now you know my dreadful secret. You don't have to tell Joe, do you?"

Swift shook her head.

"I shan't tell him," she said, "for the simple reason that I have no evidence that the pictures ever existed. Stella Dover did destroy them. She kept her word."

Chapter 18

Swift felt strangely conscious that someone was watching her closely as she made her way back to her car. Perhaps she was just being paranoid after the shock of receiving the threatening note. She glanced around as casually as she could without giving any potential stalker the pleasure of seeing she was rattled.

There were several people within sight, mostly on the move. Probably, anyone watching her would be fairly stationary. A couple of men were possibles. They strolled off casually in opposite directions the moment Swift looked round.

She didn't get a very good look at them but memorised such of their faces, hair style and clothing that she could.

Swift reached the car, opened the door and took the opportunity to look round again. The two men had vanished. Other people seemed to be going about their own business innocently.

The detective sergeant climbed in and set off on the road towards Ulceby Cross. No one followed her from the market square as she turned left onto the main road through Alford. She drove carefully at 30mph along what was, after all, a fairly narrow meandering road in a busy small town.

There was still no one following her as she reached the edge of the built-up area. Swift laughed at her own paranoia and relaxed. Suddenly, climbing the hill past Wells, she realised that a car was indeed coming up behind her at some speed. She hadn't been looking in the rear view mirror as she should have done. Indeed, it was the sound of the revved engine that alerted her. It sounded really souped up.

Swift kept a steady pace. She was not going to show weakness. She would force the driver to come up behind her, as it would be impossible to overtake safely while the road meandered through a wooded area.

However, the following car slowed as soon as it got within

striking distance and, if anything, began to fall back. Swift took a deep breath and kept a steady pace. Given the turns in the road, it was dangerous to look in the rear view mirror for more than a couple of seconds.

Two men were in the front seats. She could not be sure whether they were the two she had spotted in Alford.

As Swift approached the roundabout at Ulceby Cross, she became aware of a third vehicle tacking on the end of the line. Because of the bends in the road she could not get a good view of it. Surely she was not being followed by two carloads.

She took a decision as she slowed for the roundabout. A lorry was edging out from the turning on her immediate right and would have precedence over the vehicle behind her if she timed it right. Swift shot out safely in front of the lorry and instead of heading south on the A16 as she had originally intended, she continued round to head north instead.

From across the roundabout she saw the first car behind her shoot out, forcing the lorry to brake sharply with a screech. It came to a halt where it blocked off the second car travelling from Alford.

The lorry driver was shouting abuse out of his open cab window at the fleeing car in front of him and was ignoring the sharp blasts on the horn from the one he was blocking off.

Swift accelerated smoothly but rapidly to the legal limit of 60mph on the single carriageway towards Louth. At least she had shaken off one of the two cars but the other one stayed in touch, although it made no immediate attempt to catch her.

Plan B, to take the first turning left and cut through towards Horncastle on minor roads, had to be abandoned. If there was to be a confrontation it had better be on a main road. Swift slowed to exactly the 40mph limit through Burwell and the car behind did likewise; she speeded back up to 60mph as she came out of the limit and the response was the same.

At the roundabout on the Louth bypass, Swift decided to settle the matter: she swung all the way round the roundabout and turned back on herself, heading south. The car behind did likewise.

There was a shallow layby on the left not far down the A16.

Swift pulled in. So did the car behind. It came to rest about 10 yards away.

Swift got out of her car and turned to face the two men who climbed out of theirs. She had not got a proper look at their faces; it was too late now. They were wearing masks and walking towards her purposefully.

Swift stood her ground. She was caught completely unawares as a car travelling northwards veered across the road at speed.

The men had not expected this either. They scrambled to get out of its path but one of the two, the man who had been the driver, was caught a heavy blow by the car's offside and thrown off his feet.

After a moment's stunned hesitation, the erstwhile passenger half carried, half dragged his companion to the car, flung open the rear offside door and bundled him screaming and moaning onto the back seat. The car engine was still running with the key in the ignition.

The former passenger then jumped into the driver's seat and drove off at speed southwards.

Only now, as the driver who had intervened backed towards her, did Swift realise that she knew the car. A couple of moments later, her boyfriend Jason stepped out.

"That idiot lorry driver blocked me off at the roundabout," Jason exclaimed as if the events of the past few seconds had never happened. "Then he got out and started going on at me when I beeped him. I thought I'd never catch you up.

"I've probably collected a speeding ticket," he added ruefully. "The camera flashed. You couldn't get it cancelled, could you?"

"No I couldn't," Swift replied indignantly. "That's the least of our worries. What the hell do you think you were playing at? You could have killed him."

"He could have killed you," Jason said simply. "It was the lesser evil."

Swift took a deep breath. Only now did the enormity of what had happened dawn on her.

"Thank you Jason," she said quietly. "But I'm afraid I'm

103

going to have to report this. You deliberately knocked him down."

"I doubt very much if he'll be lodging a complaint," Jason replied calmly. "If he does, he'll have to explain what he was doing chasing after you with a mask on. I've heard of a murder trial with no body but I doubt if you'll get a road accident with no victim."

Jason was right. It has highly unlikely that a complaint would be made. On the other hand, Swift had taken the precaution of memorising the number plate of the car that had followed her. It was scribbled on a piece of paper in her car. It was the best lead she had into the murky world of Oscar Dover.

"What on earth are you doing here anyway?" she demanded. "Why aren't you at work? Don't tell me you've been fired."

"I was worried about you," Jason said. "I've got a couple of days off in lieu of all the overtime I've been working. I've been following you. I knew you needed looking after."

This was not a road that Swift wanted to go down. It was bad enough being patronised by male colleagues. She certainly wasn't going to be patronised by her boyfriend. Besides, she was completely taken aback by the first bit of Jason's last remark.

"You've been working overtime?" she asked incredulously. "I thought you were having an affair."

"An affair?" Jason responded with equal astonishment. "Why on earth would I have an affair when I've got you?"

Chapter 19

Detective Inspector Paul Amos took an internal phone call at his desk in the office he shared with the Chief Constable's personal assistant David. It was Detective Sergeant Juliet Swift asking if he could find an excuse to pop down to CID urgently.

Amos put the phone back on its cradle with a feigned sigh.

"Paperwork," he lied to David. "Shouldn't take long."

"Of course," David said genially. "It has to be done."

David was well aware that Amos thought most of the paperwork did not have to be done, hence the inspector's pretence that he was going unwillingly. David also knew that Sir Robert Fletcher was very keen on completing paperwork and had even installed Jennifer to see that it was done, so he could not discourage Amos from fulfilling this duty.

Like Amos, David suspected without any real evidence that Jennifer might be Sir Robert's spy in CID.

"I don't think we can do any more today anyway," David said. "Schools are packing up for the day."

He was anxious to keep Amos onside. Getting the schools to cooperate with the education project, David's side of the operation, was the easier bit. Amos had the tougher task of instilling enthusiasm into police ranks.

Most officers had assumed that prevarication would save them. They reckoned that the project would inevitably come to a premature halt, like the other projects that Fletcher had embarked on over the years. They were reluctantly accepting that this one had legs.

Amos ambled down the stairs to CID to avoid the chance of bumping into Fletcher in the lift. He hoped that David would not check with Jennifer and find out that the call had not been from her.

Swift was surprised that Amos had extricated himself from the top floor so quickly. She had sent her boyfriend Jason off home with the promise that she would soon join him for a romantic evening. If push came to shove, no one could say that Jason had left the scene of an accident without reporting it to a police officer.

Amos and Swift made their way into Amos's office. They didn't bother to sit down.

Swift gave a quick summary of what had happened on her way back from Alford.

"You've stirred up a hornet's nest," Amos said, stating the obvious. "Juliet, you're in some danger. This clearly goes way beyond whether Oscar Dover was murdered or not. The threatening letter sent to your home was no bluff. You have to report this."

"And have it taken out of my hands?" Swift said testily. "I've put a lot of work into this and I'm close to something big. Once I tell a senior officer it will be taken out of my hands. It's my big case."

"Tell you what," Amos said. "Go home and sleep on it. If anyone reports the accident, it will be out of your hands anyway."

After Amos had left, Swift decided not to sleep on it after all. She checked ownership of the number plate of the car that had tailed her. It was assigned to a vehicle of the correct make and colour and registered to a prominent Lincolnshire landowner whose house resembled a mansion.

Swift knew because, as a young police constable, she had been on the abortive raid that followed a very reliable drugs tip-off. The building was at the end of a long drive that began at an occupied gatehouse and meandered through parkland. The mansion was completely clear of anything incriminating when the police vehicles raced up.

There had been no way of knowing whether the owner was warned by the occupant of the gatehouse or whether the police convoy had been spotted en route. The vehicles would have been clearly visible for best part of a mile.

Swift, however, suspected that the warning had come from within Lincolnshire police headquarters. If there had been drugs on the premises, the place was cleared remarkably quickly. Swift was too junior at the time to be in the firing line but those higher up the ladder had been hauled over the coals. The building, and its owner, had been off limits ever since.

She decided, therefore, to contact the Vice Squad at Scotland Yard. They seemed decidedly interested in the details Swift provided. I won't hold my breath, she thought. Time to go home and pay Jason some attention.

The following morning, though, the car park at Lincolnshire police HQ at Nettleham was unusually crowded. Some vehicles were parked inconsiderately, further restricting the available space. As Swift entered the rear door of the building after finding a parking slot with some difficulty, she discovered why. The place was crawling with Vice Squad detectives.

Swift realised with horror what she had unleashed. Why hadn't she taken Amos's advice and slept on it? To make matters worse, the Chief Constable had just arrived to find a strange car in his clearly labelled parking space, the only one that was wide enough to take his Rolls-Royce.

Sir Robert stormed into HQ shouting so loudly that the whole building could hear him. Swift had never known him to be so angry. Nor had she heard him use such strong language before. Even the Vice Squad visitors were stunned into silence.

A pause in the tirade followed, punctuated by the clank of machinery as the Chief Constable took the lift to the top floor. Moments later David was despatched down the stairs to sort out what was going on.

Amos, who had arrived earlier than usual that morning because he was due to visit a school in Gainsborough as part of the educational project and was thus on the top floor well out of the melee, had missed the arrival of the invading horde and was completely bemused at this turn of events.

Sir Robert glanced at the rapidly departing figure of David, taking the stairs noisily two or three at a time, then turned back to Amos with a dark look.

"I would normally suspect you of being behind whatever is going on," Fletcher said angrily. "You're responsible for most things that go wrong in this place. But on this occasion I can see you are as baffled as I am."

Amos was slightly relieved. Here was something to distract Sir Robert from the education programme, something that might cause him to lose interest at last. It was a particularly good sign that David had been assigned to another task, however briefly.

Such a respite was not accorded to Swift, who very soon found herself in the Chief Constable's office.

She could tell he was really angry. The veins were standing out on his neck.

"Where do I start?" he demanded. "You think it's all right to call in the Vice Squad? You're only a detective sergeant. These things go up to a senior officer. And when were you thinking of telling me that a pack of wolves was descending on us?"

"I didn't call them in, sir," Swift answered indignantly. Amos, she knew, found it easier to take the line of least resistance and let Sir Robert's temper run its course. As a female in a mainly man's world she felt the need to stand her ground.

"Well they say you called them. They didn't just come for personal amusement. Half of them don't even know where Lincolnshire is."

"I called them for information. I didn't ask them to pay a visit. I'm as shocked as you are to see them."

"Information? Information?" the Chief Constable nearly exploded. "_You_ gave _them_ information. That's the way the Vice Squad works. They don't tell you anything. It's a one way street. Which is why these things go to a senior officer.

"Well, the damage is done now. They're here and we'll have to make the best of it. You just keep well out of it. And that's an order."

There was worse to come. In the passage on the way to the stairs she passed Detective Sergeant Gerry Burnside walking purposefully towards the Chief Constable's office.

Chapter 20

"Hello, Juliet," Burnside said cheerfully, his face breaking into a broad grin. "You're in on it, then. Good for you."

Swift stopped, looking puzzled. Burnside was based in Boston and Swift was happy to keep the 40-odd miles between them. He was married but took any opportunity to persistently flirt with any younger female colleagues including, on the rare occasions their paths had crossed, with Swift herself.

Burnside was turning into a middle aged louche whose attraction for the opposite sex was in terminal decline. Only he seemed to be unaware of it.

Seeing him at HQ was as a bit of a shock, especially coming immediately after her unpleasant encounter with the Chief Constable.

"Can't stop to chat now," Burnside said, ignoring the lack of response. He was used to this type of reaction which, far from putting him off, was a challenge to try harder. "I'll talk to you downstairs when I've finished with the big fellow."

Not if I can get out before Fletcher has finished with you, Swift thought as Burnside vanished into the Chief Constable's office. She could just catch the sound of Sir Robert greeting the Boston detective like some long-lost friend.

On the stairs, Swift was hit by a sickening thought. Had Fletcher summoned Burnside to take over _her_ case?

She paused mid-flight. Surely that wasn't possible. Fletcher had only just found out about the Vice Squad's visit. There hadn't been time. Boston to Lincoln, with blues and twos blaring and flashing, could not be done in less than half an hour even in the lightest traffic. Swift knew. She'd attempted it.

So Burnside must have left Boston before Fletcher discovered his HQ was littered with Vice Squad detectives.

Yet it was surely no coincidence that Burnside was being greeted with enthusiasm in inverse proportion to her own ignominious dressing down, and immediately afterwards at that.

Swift suddenly realised she was losing valuable escape time. She hastened back to CID, only to be delayed further as one of the detective constables on her team reported that Gainsborough police station had made two arrests in the rural burglaries case that she had been assigned to and which had provided the cover for her to continue probing Oscar Dover's death. Some of the missing goods had been recovered.

"That's great," Swift said. "Sounds like they've got it all sewn up. I'm more than happy to let them take over the case. Pass on all the stuff we've got on it to them."

She was pretty bored with the case anyway. The only trouble was that there was now no excuse to leave HQ. Nor was there time, for Burnside was bounding into CID, smiling broadly. At least someone was having a good day.

Burnside made a beeline for her.

"Juliet," he said, "can we have a quiet word. I gather Amos's office is currently available."

Can this get any worse, Swift wondered. Burnside, her equal as a detective sergeant, was commandeering her own boss's office, apparently with the blessing of the Chief Constable.

"Please," Burnside added, firmly but with a hint of pleading.

Swift led the way, partly to look as if she was in control and partly because it would be demeaning to allow Burnside to hold the door open for her.

"Let's get down to business," Burnside said as soon as he had closed the door. "I don't know if you are aware of the fact that I'm Lincolnshire liaison officer with the Yard's Vice Squad."

Swift didn't know. She doubted if anyone knew apart from Burnside and, presumably, the Chief Constable. Burnside had probably been given the role as a sop at some point on the assumption that it would never actually come to anything.

"It hasn't amounted to much," Burnside admitted. "Until now, that is. This is big. As soon as the Vice Squad got your call they were onto me straight away."

"Oh great," Swift said. "I do the dirty work, get threatened and they hand it straight over to you. I suppose I'm being sent out on traffic duty while you big boys have all the fun."

"Doesn't have to be like that," Burnside replied. "Who knows about what you've been up to? In particular, who here at HQ knows about the owner of the car that the goons were driving?"

"Nobody here knows about the goons," Swift said.

Having avoided mentioning the key presence of her boyfriend at the incident when she rang the Vice Squad, she saw no point in mentioning it now. As far as she knew the goons, as Burnside called them, had apparently not reported that Jason had deliberately driven into one of them, so there was no sense in bringing it up.

"What about your enquiries into the indecent photographs?" Burnside asked.

"I haven't mentioned them either," Swift said. "DC Susan Smith has a vague inkling but that's all."

"Good," Burnside said. He glanced round. Amos's office had windows and a glass door facing out into CID. He could see that no one was nearby in hearing distance.

"I don't know whether you're aware of this, and I probably shouldn't say, but as you're on the team you ought to know. We're mounting a raid as soon as we can get the necessary vehicles. Don't tell anyone it's Joseph Grainger who's the target.

"You're probably aware he's a big cheese in the county set. He got raided once before and when nothing was found apart from one out-of-date road tax disc there was hell to pay."

"I know. I was there," Swift said. "What exactly do you mean, I'm on the team? What team?"

"For God's sake, Juliet, don't play at being naïve. I know you're not stupid. You're on the raid. It's your case after all. As a matter of fact, I insisted on it. I am the Lincolnshire liaison officer, after all. Don't worry, Sir Robert's approved it. He seemed almost pleased about it. I think he has a soft spot for you."

This was a mixed blessing as far as Swift was concerned. At least she wasn't off the case altogether but Burnside would get all the credit. What was more, he would be in a position to patronise her and press his unwanted attentions.

The option to refuse was taken out of her hands as the door to Amos's office swung open, catching both officers unawares, even though the tall, burly man in his 40s who now entered must have walked through CID in full view.

He acknowledged Burnside with barely a nod.

"DS Juliet Swift, I take it," he said, extending his hand. "Commander Reg Blake, Vice Squad. You ready to go? You're in my car."

Swift shook the proffered hand and glanced momentarily at Burnside, who seemed not the slightest bit put out.

"I'm ready," Swift replied.

She wasn't sure if the team of detectives she was effectively running in Amos's absence actually had anything to do but that wasn't her worry any more. Orders were orders.

Burnside was already bounding out of the door and across CID like a sprinter jumping the gun.

"Walk straight out without looking at anyone," Blake said, "but don't attract attention by rushing. Just follow me."

Blake led the way to the carpark. Other plain clothes officers whom Swift had never seen before, along with three or four uniformed ones from Lincoln, fell in behind as if popping magically out of the woodwork. It was like a scene from a well choreographed musical but without the music.

Swift glanced round the carpark as she followed Blake to the lead car. There was no sign of Burnside.

"You can ride shotgun," Blake remarked casually. "I don't like the excitement."

A driver, whom Swift vaguely recognised as a local officer, was in the driving seat with the engine running. She got in the front passenger seat and Blake sat alone in the back. As they edged forward to the carpark exit, Swift noted half a dozen other vehicles filling up with the officers who had followed them.

"Blues only," Blake told the driver. So it was to be flashing lights but no sirens, Swift thought. Are we in a hurry or not? Blake, however, seemed content with brisk rather than frantic progress towards the rural mansion that was the home of Joseph Grainger.

Swift glanced in the wing mirror. The cars following in convoy also had lights flashing.

"Tell me when we're about a couple of miles from the entrance," Blake said suddenly as they sped along the main road.

"Will do," Swift said.

Silence resumed. Blake didn't seem to be a man who indulged in talk for the sake of it.

Some minutes of silence later, Swift said: "We're getting close."

"Lights off," Blake said curtly.

Swift saw in the wing mirror that the following cars took their cue to turn off their flashing blue lights one after the other like a row of dominoes.

There were two or three minutes of further silence until the moment the lead car turned into the start of the drive to Grainger's property.

"Go, go, go," Blake barked suddenly. Blue lights and siren came on immediately and the car screeched forward past the gatehouse, pushing Swift back into her seat. A bit of warning wouldn't have come amiss, she thought, but she didn't complain. The thrill was exhilarating.

Blake certainly enjoyed dramatics.

"Stop," he shouted as his car reached the front of the house. The vehicle skidded to a sharp halt on the gravel. It was a miracle that none of the following cars shunted into each other.

Even so, the commander was out of the door before his car was fully stationary. Officers scrambled out of the other cars as if it were a competition to avoid being last to hit the ground running.

Blake waved wildly to the occupants of the last two cars to rush round the back of the building to prevent anyone escaping or removing evidence. He himself was running up the stone steps to the front of the building.

Swift and a dozen officers followed. She looked for

Burnside. There was still no sign of him. She stood watching the other officers hurry past her and through the grand front door that Blake had flung open with a melodramatic flourish, a sickening feeling hitting the pit of her stomach.

No wonder Burnside had insisted in having her on the team. He knew the raid would find nothing and she would be tainted with the failure. It was her punishment for spurning him in the past. Was Burnside, then, the police insider who tipped off Grainger?

It was too late now.

Swift bounded up the stone steps in pursuit of the last officer and in through the now closing front door. Those in first clearly had had their orders, for they were fanning out, some up the flowing marble stairway immediately in front of them and others either side of it into rooms and passages.

This had been well planned by someone with knowledge of the building. Someone like Burnside who could easily have found the layout from the police files of the earlier raid and used the information to cover his role as Grainger's insider in the force.

"There you are," Blake said to Swift as he finished waving his troops into battle. "I thought I'd lost you."

Swift immediately recognised Grainger, though it was several years since she had last seen him in the flesh. His face often adorned the pages of Lincolnshire newspapers, usually being lauded as a charity fundraiser.

He was standing in the middle of the hall with his arms folded, not in surprise at events taking place around him but with a look of mild amusement on his face.

Another man stood nearby. It could have been one of the two who had threatened her on the road from Ulceby Cross to Louth – he was the right height and sturdy build of the man who had dragged his stricken accomplice back into the car – but she couldn't be sure, having not seen his face.

He showed no recognition of, or indeed particular interest in, Swift.

Blake was attempting to make Grainger look at the search warrant he was brandishing. Grainger ostentatiously looked at the signature of the magistrate then walked away into a side room followed by the other man.

There was a cry from the top of the stairs.

"You'd better come, Sir," a uniformed officer called to Blake.

"Come on, Sergeant," Blake said to Swift. "Let's see what we've found."

Disappointingly, however, it was not evidence of wrongdoing. It was a man lying on his back on a bed, sweating profusely and groaning as he gripped and kneaded the pillow.

A pair of crutches was propped up against the wall next to the bedhead.

"Painkillers," the man on the bed gasped. "Get me my painkillers. They're on the bedside table."

Blake picked up a small medicine bottle standing next to a glass of water and containing capsules. He looked at the label.

"These are morphine," he said sharply. "Where did you get them?"

He showed Swift the label. There was no identification of the pharmacy that had dispensed them.

The man on the bed was going frantic. He attempted to snatched the bottle from the Commander's hand, but Blake drew it back out of reach smartly, leaving the invalid to slump back with more shrieks of pain.

"For pity's sake," the wretched man gasped. "Give me my painkillers."

He was practically sobbing with the agony. Blake was unmoved.

"Are you under medical supervision?" Blake demanded. "Who's treating you?"

"The painkillers," was the only response.

Blake relented and handed him the bottle and the tumbler of water that had been standing next to it. The man on the bed fumbled to unscrew the cap of the bottle, spilling the water and subsequently the capsules onto the duvet, then swallowed three capsules greedily in one gulp before collapsing back into a prone position again with a loud sigh of relief.

"I'm getting you an ambulance," Blake said. "You should be

in hospital."

The Commander picked up the telephone extension that also stood on the bedside table and dialled 999. The uniformed officer was instructed to stand guard until the ambulance arrived.

"Don't let anyone try to move him," Blake ordered.

Then he said to Swift: "I shouldn't have let him have the capsules. I should have made him tell us how he got the injuries first. He looks as if someone's run him down with a car."

Blake and Swift returned to the foot of the staircase. In the minutes before the ambulance turned up, the other officers reported back one by one.

As Swift feared, no one had found any incriminating evidence. Two officers returned carrying a couple of desktop personal computers but no compact discs.

"Bag up the computers," Blake said. "I don't suppose they were stupid enough to have left anything on them but you never know."

Grainger and the other man with him came out of the side room on the ground floor.

"I'd like them back as soon as you've finished messing about with them," Grainger said. "They've got the estate accounts on them. Don't lose anything."

Blake was taking it all very calmly given that the exercise was rapidly turning into a disaster. She could hardly hope that Sir Robert Fletcher would be so phlegmatic.

"You've got everything backed up on discs, I take it," Blake said easily.

Grainger merely glared at him.

Blake showed remarkable sangfroid in the face of a distinct lack of evidence. An awful lot of man and womanpower had been expended in this exercise and although most of the likely waste was down to the Vice Squad, Swift had an uneasy feeling that she would make a very convenient scapegoat back at Lincolnshire Police Headquarters.

At least her boyfriend Jason was earning. He could look after her for a change if she lost her job.

A vehicle's horn beeped twice. A Transit van came round the side of the house followed by a couple of police cars.

To Swift's surprise, she recognised the van driver. It was Gerry Burnside.

The detective sergeant from Boston leapt out with a broad grin on his face.

"All present and correct, Sir," he called cheerfully to Blake. "Worked a treat."

Grainger had come out of his luxurious home and was now standing at the top of the steps sweeping down from the front door. The colour was draining visibly from his face.

"Once bitten, twice shy," Burnside called to him gloatingly. "You didn't think we'd fall for that stunt a second time, did you?"

The light was beginning to dawn on Swift. She could see two men she did not recognise, each accompanied by a uniformed police officer, sitting in the back seat of the two police cars following Burnside. Both men looked crestfallen and were gazing down at the floor, studiously avoiding looking at Grainger.

"No wonder you disappeared," Swift said to Burnside with a grudging admiration. "You cut off the escape route."

"Yup," Burnside replied smugly. "Guilty as charged."

The Boston detective sergeant stood on one side with Swift as he explained.

"I was a constable wet behind the ears on the last raid on these premises. We all knew what had happened but we all felt powerless to do anything about it. I came back the following weekend and drove all the way round the outside of the estate. There had to be another way out – one they could use to evacuate the building when they were tipped off we were coming to get them.

"It wasn't easy to find, I can tell you. There wasn't anything on any of the maps of the area, not even on the largest scale ones. On the third circuit I finally spotted a narrow track that led into a farmyard. The buildings were derelict and behind an old barn was open land with the unmistakeable marks of car, not tractor, tyres. They'd come back with the stuff once they knew the coast was clear.

"I took a stroll up to the top of the hill and there was the manor house nestling down in the valley. So this morning we could lie in wait out of sight of the house until they were coming up through the gap in a copse.

"We had 'em surrounded before they knew what had hit them. And the best part is they'd loaded up all the incriminating stuff neatly for us."

"Come on, Burnside," Blake interrupted jovially. "Time to get back to HQ. The real work starts now."

Chapter 21

Det Sgt Juliet Swift was the only officer not to be in jubilant mood as the cavalcade made its way at speed back to Lincolnshire police HQ at Nettleham with sirens blazing and blue lights flashing.

The big imponderable was what Chief Constable Sir Robert Fletcher's reaction would be to the startling events of the morning. Not only would he have his headquarters crawling with Vice Squad personnel but he would have to concede at least one other police station to them. Swift realised that the suspects would be split for their interviews.

There was no doubt who would get the blame for the inconvenience.

She had lost control of her own case. Conceding to the Vice Squad was bearable – after all, she was the one who had alerted them in the first place. It was seeing a fellow detective sergeant, Gerry Burnside, taking her rightful place that stuck in the craw.

Nor would she now have scope to pursue the mysterious death of Oscar Dover, a case she had invested so much time and effort into.

The best policy would be to avoid Sir Robert for as long as possible and give him time to get used to the situation so Swift resolved to stick close to Blake for as long as possible. They'd got on pretty well in the short time they had known each other and at least Blake would be going back to London sooner or later.

This proved easier than expected. Blake wanted Swift to join him in questioning Grainger and was keen to get on with it. Grainger, looking decidedly shellshocked, declined to request a solicitor to represent him.

We know he's got a contact in the police, Swift wondered. Is it someone sufficiently high up to get him off?

Blake was a stickler for having interviews properly recorded.

Swift had been used to a more relaxed attitude from her Chief Constable but she knew that Blake was right and it was his call.

"Interview commencing at 12.15pm," Blake intoned flatly. "Present: Commander Blake, Vice Squad, and Detective Sergeant Juliet Swift of Lincolnshire Constabulary.

"Please identify yourself," he said to Grainger, who complied grudgingly.

"Mr Grainger," Blake resumed. "As you know, we have taken a quantity of photographs and documents from your premises this morning plus two word processors. Would you like to tell me what we will find when we sort through them?"

"No I wouldn't," Grainger said testily. "Like to. Anyway, you didn't get them from my home so how should I know?"

"They were on your land when they were seized, in the possession of your employees. Why don't you save us all a lot of time?"

"No comment."

A member of the Vice Squad entered the room and casually tossed a pile of photographs onto the table in front of Blake.

"Try these for starters," the officer remarked casually. "We've taken fingerprints off them. They were well thumbed through."

Blake spread a few of the pictures on the desk top. They were all pornographic and most were naked children with adults of both sexes.

Despite his years in the Vice Squad, Blake looked quite shocked. He nodded to the officer, who withdrew, then turned to Grainger and said coldly: "Children. Do you find them sexy?"

"No comment," came the flat reply.

"When and where were these pictures taken?"

"No comment."

"Who took them? Who are the children? Who are the adults in the photographs? How did they come to be in your possession?"

Each question elicited a shrug and a "No comment."

"I'm getting hungry," Blake said. He was also getting

irritable and impatient. "It's been a long time since breakfast. Why don't you do us a favour and start cooperating. We'll find everything in your files anyway."

"Why are you asking me, then?" Grainger asked with sudden defiance.

Swift felt uneasy. Grainger was taking this far too calmly, given the quantity of evidence that had been seized. He really believes someone quite high in Lincolnshire Police will get him off, she thought.

Blake glanced at Swift. It was a clear signal to see if she had anything to ask.

This was a welcome change. Most male officers would have ignored her. Even Paul Amos, her immediate superior, preferred to ask all the questions, although he took the same attitude whether in the presence of a male or female junior officer.

On the other hand, Swift had been caught out by the speed of developments so far and what she wanted to ask Grainger about was not the pornography as such, which the Vice Squad would deal with, but what happened to Oscar Dover.

She therefore shook her head almost imperceptibly and let the opportunity pass.

Commander Blake's gamble of letting Grainger stew for an hour worked badly. It gave Grainger time to decide he wanted legal representation after all, which delayed matters for a further hour while the solicitor made the journey from Louth to Lincolnshire police HQ.

Then there was a further hold-up as the solicitor understandably requested a brief private chat with his client. When the interview finally resumed it soon became clear that Grainger would not be cooperating with any line of enquiry.

Swift pressed him on the issue of Oscar Dover without success. Instead, Grainger seemed no longer rattled by the mere mention of the name.

Blake soon took over the pointless questioning. At least he now had more information to work on, his team having rummaged through more boxes and files seized from Grainger's home.

"Mr Grainger," Blake said, "We are now making arrests in various parts of the country based on information found in your files. What do you have to say?"

Grainger had nothing to say.

"Quite a network you were part of," Blake remarked. "They'll all be impressed when they find that you were the weak link in the chain."

Grainger looked silently unimpressed but, just in case, the solicitor put a restraining hand on his client's arm to discourage him from being goaded.

"Some of these names have been on our watch list for quite a while," Blake continued. "You've just done us a big favour. And one name we haven't come across before: Tony Folkestone. Care to tell us about him?"

Grainger did not care to say anything, though he gave a short, involuntary smirk.

The Vice Squad commander leaned forward and continued with a menacing tone: "This isn't amusing and you're going down for a very long time so you may as well tell us about him and save us all a lot of bother. He's obviously the linchpin in all this."

No amount of wheedling, threatening or cajoling would elicit any clues as to the elusive Tony Folkestone.

Swift had rather switched off, especially as she had no real input to make and the questioning was getting nowhere anyway.

Suddenly a thought struck her.

"Tony ... Oscar," she said. "Two acting awards. "Folkestone ... Dover. Two ports in Kent. Tony Folkestone is Oscar Dover, isn't he? Not a very subtle code name, is it? Couldn't you do better than that?"

Grainger was finally stung into breaking his silence.

"It was a joke," he said patronisingly. "We didn't care who worked it out because it didn't matter. Oscar Dover wasn't a lynchpin. He was just an errand boy. A very useful errand boy, I don't deny. In fact, it was a real inconvenience when he died suddenly. It meant finding some other mug to replace him."

"I advise you not to say anything further," the solicitor said urgently. "This isn't helping."

Blake rapidly lost interest in Oscar Dover/Tony Folkestone.

"He's not much use to us if he's dead," he remarked to Swift after the interview was again suspended.

"We don't need to bother about him anymore. We've got tons of stuff on Grainger and dozens of others. This is really big. I'll see you get your fair share of the credit."

Swift had no doubt that at that moment he meant it but she knew it was an empty promise. She would gradually become peripheral to the pornography inquiry.

There was no let-up for the Vice Squad that weekend but DS Swift's presence at Lincolnshire police headquarters was not required. She wasn't sorry, as it gave her and her boyfriend Jason a chance to rekindle their strained romance.

Swift returned to Nettleham on Monday morning in good spirits. The place seemed strangely quiet.

"Where is everybody?" she asked Jennifer as civilly as she could manage, given her reluctance to ask the CID's little helper anything at all.

"All gone to London," Jennifer replied brightly.

It further annoyed Swift that she could never manage to break Jennifer's glassy exterior.

"Sir Robert would like a word," Jennifer added.

Sir Robert, for once, did not wait to summon Swift to the top floor. A few moments later, before Swift had hardly had time to plonk her bag on her desk, the Chief Constable appeared in CID. His spirits were evidently much higher than Swift's.

"They've carted Grainger and his crew back to London," he beamed. "We've got our headquarters back!"

"That's good, Sir," Swift answered politely.

"It certainly is," Fletcher continued. "Remain ready to go to London if they need you. Gerry Burnside is there already. Good to see you two getting on so well. Remember, don't get involved in anything big here in Lincoln in case you're needed at short notice."

"That's fine, Sir," Swift assured him. "I'll make sure I don't."

"In any case," Fletcher said cautiously. "there's a pile of

paperwork arising from all this. I suppose some of the aversion to paper has rubbed off onto you from Amos but it has to be done. Commander Blake of the Vice Squad wants full statements from you on all your dealings with Grainger. Jennifer has the stuff."

Fletcher turned abruptly on his heels and left the room before Swift had time to react.

"It's on your desk," Jennifer said.

Chapter 22

That lunchtime Amos found himself in the Lincolnshire Police HQ canteen when he came across Doug Daley. Their paths crossed occasionally because Daley was in forensics and Amos called on his expertise from time to time. Although the two were on amicable terms, they were far from bosom friends.

However, Amos was anxious for a change of company. Being enclosed in one room with David for most of the day would have been bad enough when the two were barely on speaking terms but at least they could have ignored each other.

Now that Amos seemed to be making a success of the Chief Constable's latest pet project, David had cast aside his suspicions of the detective inspector and was starting to regard him as a worthy colleague who could be trusted and even admired. Having to make pleasant conversation was worse than silence.

Daley was already seated alone at a table.

"Mind if I join you Doug?" Amos asked pleasantly. Then, for want of anything better to say, he added: "There's something I want to run past you."

"No, I'm not joining your grand project," Daley said almost aggressively. "I didn't join forensics to wander round schools telling snotty nosed kids to get a life."

Amos had indeed nursed hopes of roping Daley in for a bit of school visiting. It would add variety to a potentially humdrum programme. However, Daley's rejection was so emphatic that he felt obliged to pretend otherwise.

"Not at all Doug, not at all," he protested. "What do you know about barium hydroxide?"

Dale raised his eyebrows quizzically.

"Who are you thinking of bumping off?" he asked drily.

"Why, is it dangerous?" Amos asked in some surprise. "I thought it was an alkali. Isn't that safe?"

"That's one way of putting it," Daley said with a chuckle. "Or you could call it a heavy metal. That sounds a lot more sinister."

"Can you poison someone with it?"

"You certainly can. It's called baryta water when you dissolve the powder. Even a tiny dose can make you feel ill – vomiting, cramps, diarrhoea. Keep dosing someone and their vital organs shut down. Only a couple of grams in one dose could be fatal."

Amos was stunned. What Daley was describing fitted what had happened to Oscar Dover perfectly and the stuff had been stolen from the school that Dover's daughters had attended.

Seeing that the inspector had lapsed deep into thought, Daley remarked jocularly: "Don't even think about it. This stuff can survive intense heat. So even if you had your victim cremated we could still find traces of it in the ashes."

Amos wasted no time in seeking out DS Juliet Swift, leaving his meal half eaten in front of a surprised Doug Daley, but before he could relay the information he had just gleaned Swift spoke first.

"Let's just have a quiet chat in your office," she said, glancing pointedly at Jennifer, who was still well within hearing distance.

Amos turned and led Swift to the inner sanctum he so hated but which he had to admit was very useful at times.

Swift closed the door behind her and deliberately stood with her back to Jennifer so the latter could not glean anything through the window from her lips or demeanour.

"I suppose you're aware that I'm helping the Vice Squad at the moment," she said.

Amos nodded.

"I don't expect that to last much longer," the detective sergeant continued, "although of course I may be called to give evidence sometime in the future."

"That'll be a long way off," Amos spoke the obvious. "As you know we don't hold trials until all the witnesses have forgotten what happened."

Swift briefly outlined the gist of the interviews with

Grainger, including his reaction to the mention of Oscar Dover's name.

"I'd still like to have one more crack at the death of Oscar Dover. I'm convinced he was bumped off by somebody and there's no shortage of possible culprits."

"You've a good feeling for this sort of thing, Juliet," Amos said. "Here's my advice. Give the pornography case your main attention as far as it's needed. That's the top priority. At least we're sure there's a crime and who committed it.

"From what you tell me, it seems unlikely that Grainger wanted Dover dead and in any case you won't have the opportunity to pursue him for it while the Vice Squad have got him. The one outside possibility is that Dover threatened to spill the beans on the porno ring and had to be silenced."

Swift thought for a moment.

"I think he was too involved in it to grass on Grainger without landing himself with a long spell in jail," she finally said. "And he doesn't seem to have been so prone to getting himself drunk that Grainger would worry he might let something slip.

"No, if Dover was done in it was almost certainly not Grainger. I'm not saying, though, that it wasn't anything to do with the dirty pictures he kept in his wallet."

"Well here's a new line of inquiry you might just be able to pick up on," Amos said. "If Oscar Dover was poisoned with the barium hydroxide that was stolen from his daughters' school, traces of it would be found in his ashes. The stuff is apparently a lot more unpleasant than I realised. I'll leave the thought with you."

Amos returned to his lonely life with David on the top floor.

Swift grabbed the phone on Amos's desk and dialled the undertaker who had handled Oscar Dover's funeral. Frank Dickinson's assistant answered the call.

"Where's Mr Dickinson?" Swift demanded

"He's at a burial at Alford Parish Church," the assistant replied cautiously, clearly disconcerted by Swift's aggressive tone.

"When will he be back?"

"In about a couple of hours, I think."

"Oscar Dover," Swift barked down the line. "It was a cremation. What happened to his ashes?"

"We collected them a couple of days ago from the crematorium," the assistant admitted in the face of Swift's barrage.

"Don't let them out of your sight," Swift ordered. "And don't let Mr Dickinson release them either if he gets back before I reach you. Understand?"

Swift didn't wait to hear if the hapless assistant understood. She slammed the phone down, returned to her desk, picked up the pile of papers that Jennifer had left on her desk and marched off with them back into Amos's office, taking petty satisfaction from not working on them where Jennifer had placed them.

She looked through what was required then started working on them at a pace she calculated would take her to about 3pm.

Swift and her boyfriend Jason had arranged to eat in Lincoln around 8pm. Jason was working late – Swift was now satisfied that this was genuine – and he was assuming that Swift would return to the home they shared and change.

She had in fact put a change of clothing into a holdall in her car boot. She would therefore have time to conduct a couple of interviews without having to endure Jason's perennial complaint that she worked too long hours.

Occasionally she emerged from the office to give instructions or guidance to a detective constable on the same team as herself, mainly to keep Jennifer guessing.

Swift knew that Jennifer always walked to the canteen for a beaker of tea at five to three. This day was no exception. Swift quickly deposited the completed paperwork onto Jennifer's desk and slipped out into the carpark, pulling her jacket on as she went.

She left no note. Jennifer presumably knew what needed doing with the forms and statements.

DS Swift raced to Alford with blue lights and siren blazing away. Even so, Frank Dickinson was sitting comfortably in his office looking slightly smug by the time she arrived. His assistant, still looking a little flustered, showed Swift through into the inner sanctum.

"I believe you were asking about Mr Oscar Dover's ashes," Dickinson said smoothly. "I'm afraid I can't help you there."

"Oh yes you can, and you will," Swift said sternly.

"You don't understand," the funeral director said unperturbed. "It's true that we collected the ashes from the crematorium but we no longer have them."

"Stella Dover?" Swift said, half question, half statement.

Dickinson nodded. Client confidentiality seemed to have gone by the board.

"They are, after all, her – ahem – property."

"When did she collect them?" Swift asked with a sinking feeling.

"Yesterday morning," came the reply. "It's not my place to say, of course, but I had the impression that Miss Dover intended to dispose of them at one of her brother's favourite spots."

Swift left the funeral parlour with her tail between her legs. It was impossible to know whether Stella Dover really had picked up the ashes the previous day or whether Dickinson had tipped her off but there was only one way to find out.

She drove the short distance to Stella Dover's house without enthusiasm. To her surprise, she found Oscar Dover's two daughters at their aunt's home.

The atmosphere between the three women was remarkably relaxed and cordial.

"We're just having a brew," Julia said cheerfully to Swift. "Do you fancy one?"

Swift ignored the offer.

Instead she turned to the aunt and said: "Your brother's ashes. Where are they?"

"We've disposed of the ashes," Stella Dover said simply. "In accordance with Oscar's wishes."

"We scattered them on the beach at Huttoft Bank," Lynn, the younger sister, chimed in solemnly. "Dad used to love parking his car there and walking along the beach. It's what he would have wanted."

"Did he say so in his will?" Swift demanded.

"He didn't have to," Julia said. "We all agreed it was the right thing to do."

There was a look of defiance in her face that got right up Swift's nose. She was tempted to point out that Julia had previously insisted that her father wanted to be buried with her mother.

"It's all very cosy in here," she said sarcastically. "Playing happy families, are we?"

"Auntie Stella is the only family we've got now," Julia replied. "Families stick together. That's what they do."

"Auntie Stella's been good to us," Lynn added. "She's helped us with Dad's ashes and drove us to the seaside to scatter them. It was our decision and she supported us. We all remembered Dad in our own way and said our goodbyes. It was lovely."

"Dare I mention the house?" Swift asked, somewhat deflated.

"It's all settled," Stella Dover said without a touch of irony. "The girls can keep it. I don't need it and I've got no children of my own. So it will stay in the family for one more generation at least."

Swift drove back to Lincoln minus siren, minus flashing lights, completely crestfallen.

Chapter 23

David was waiting anxiously for Detective Sergeant Swift when she arrived at Lincolnshire Police Headquarters the following morning.

"Sir Robert wants to see you," he said before Swift had hardly hard time to enter the building.

"He's in a good mood," David reassured her hastily.

The Chief Constable was, indeed, a happy man, so happy that for once he remembered Swift's first name correctly.

"Juliet," he said warmly. "Do come in. All well with the Vice Squad?"

David hovered uncertainly in the doorway, not wishing to be drawn in but wanting to keep abreast of developments.

"As far as I know, Sir," Swift replied politely. "I understand Detective Sergeant Burnside is liaising."

"Yes, yes," Fletcher acknowledged with a wave of his hand. "The question is how we're going to capitalise on this. Lincolnshire has led the way in stamping out a particularly nasty blight on the country as a whole. We should turn this into a campaign."

Fine, Swift thought, just as long as I don't get caught up in it. At least if this replaces the education project I'll get Amos back.

"I should think the best person to help with that would be Detective Sergeant Burnside," she said. It would probably mean him coming to HQ more often with his unwanted attentions for the ladies but that would be the lesser evil compared with getting roped in herself.

"As long as you don't mind, Juliet," Fletcher said amiably. "It was you who started all this, after all, and I didn't want you to feel you were being pushed out."

David uncharacteristically disappeared from the doorway. He normally wanted to be hovering whenever the Chief Constable was talking to junior members of staff and he most certainly needed to be in on the start of any new project, since he always bore the brunt of Sir Robert's periodic whims.

However, Fletcher usually let one project die a natural death, as he gradually got bored with the subject, well before launching a new enthusiasm.

Caught between the devil and the deep blue sea, David chose the devil in the form of Detective Inspector Paul Amos. At least they were on the same side in wanting an end to the education project and having to work together, so any change of tack affected them both equally.

If push came to shove, David had the Chief Constable's ear and could put the blame onto Amos should there subsequently be any perceived shortcomings.

The detective inspector was in the room that had been allocated for the two of them to work together in uneasy cooperation. Amos was struggling with The Times crossword, which he hastily put back under a pile of papers listing details of schools in the county.

"I don't know what's going to happen next," David blurted out.

Amos shrugged his shoulders.

"None of us do," he replied cautiously. "Can you be more specific?"

"We seem to be grinding to a halt," David said sadly. "The schools are well into the exams season and it's getting hard to find new ones to visit."

Amos knew this perfectly well but it didn't particularly worry him. Finding the schools was David's problem; Amos's was to supply the officers to take part. Nonetheless, he was thoroughly bored and welcomed the diversion.

"Do you think we should wind down and reconvene in the autumn when the schools return," Amos asked genially. It was important to push the responsibility back onto David.

"In any case, there will be a six week break for the summer hols. It's a case of when Sir Robert will accept we should suspend operations and you are closer to the Chief Constable than I am."

Both men knew that once the project went into limbo it

would be dropped for good, an outcome that they both fervently wanted.

David pondered the situation. How far could he trust Amos?

"It's not just that," David said hesitatingly. "Sir Robert is talking about launching a campaign against child pornography. Where will that leave us?"

Amos sat up sharply. He and David were both aware where that left them: with an opportunity to get shut of the schools project once and for all.

Indecisive David could not be trusted with this. Amos would have to tackle the Chief Constable head on, preferably without letting slip that he knew about the new project.

"Look David," he said reassuringly. "It's not fair to put everything onto you. Why don't I have a word with Sir Robert? He'll understand the situation."

David looked doubtful. Even he could recognise hypocrisy when it stared him in the face so blatantly.

"There's another problem," the unhappy personal assistant admitted. "I'm due a fortnight's holiday starting this weekend. It was booked ages before all this came up. I've got a family reunion on and I don't know if Sir Robert will remember he promised me I could go."

"Don't worry," Amos said firmly, hiding his surprise that David actually had a family of any kind. "Leave it to me. I'll get it all sorted. You will get your holiday. You shall go to the ball, Cinderella."

Amos rose to his feet before David could raise any objections.

"No time like the present," he said casually as he left the room.

Fletcher's door was open. Swift had already returned to CID. Amos gave only the briefest of taps on it and walked in without bidding for the first time in his career. Sir Robert, who was putting a book in its place on a shelf, turned round.

"I know you've got more important things to think about at the moment," Amos said firmly before the Chief Constable could speak, "but David and I are going to have to suspend the schools project until the autumn."

"Yes, yes," Fletcher said absentmindedly. "Yes, fine."

"In any case," Amos continued, confident that the Chief Constable was hardly listening. "I gather you promised David the next couple of weeks off and I don't see any need to disrupt your arrangement. So now seems an ideal time to break for the summer."

"Yes, indeed," Sir Robert replied without a glimmer of interest. "Quite so. Tell David that's fine. I shall have work for him to do when he comes back refreshed. And CID will be pleased to see you back.

"Close the door on your way out."

Meanwhile, Swift had taken a walk out into the carpark to think things through and try to decide, unsuccessfully, what to do next about Oscar Dover.

She returned to CID resigned to slipping back into the old routine. Talking of the old routine, Amos was in the department, chatting amiably to the CID's beautiful assistant Jennifer.

"Juliet," Amos exclaimed, breaking off readily enough from the lure of the blonde bombshell. "You've been having all the excitement, I hear. I'm coming back to CID. The Chief Constable has suspended the education project for the summer and I gather we may have a new project by the time schools resume."

"Don't let's talk about that," Swift replied gloomily, not caring that Jennifer could hear and might report back to Sir Robert. "I may get roped into that one. I just hope that by then Fletcher will have forgotten all about me."

"OK," Amos said. "Let's talk about something far more pleasing. I'm taking next week off as annual leave. I've managed to find a hotel room in Sorrento and picked up a couple of last minute tickets flying from East Midlands airport to Naples. I'm sure if you've waited this long you can wait another week without me."

"See Naples and die," Jennifer said with a smile.

"They say Manchester has the same effect," Amos replied lightly.

Amos and Swift moved away from Jennifer's desk, Amos

more reluctantly than Swift.

"If you're going to be missing for a bit longer," Swift said, "I'm going to have one last crack at Oscar Dover."

"Up to you," Amos said as a parting shot before he walked out of HQ and into a holiday in Italy. "But you should work on the basis that you've only got next week to nail it."

Chapter 24

The week turned effectively into just two days. As soon as she arrived at Lincolnshire Police Headquarters on Monday morning, DS Swift was informed by Jennifer, the office manager, that she was required in London for a couple of days to help with the investigation into the pornography ring that she had uncovered.

This was particularly annoying. Had she been rung at home on the west side of Lincoln she could have gone straight to the station to the south of the city centre instead of trailing across to Nettleham, caught an early train to get to Scotland Yard at lunchtime and chopped a day off the trip.

As it was she had to get back home, shove some clothes into a holdall and catch a later train changing at Nottingham, which meant it would be late afternoon and the day wasted by the time she arrived. Thus two days in London would translate into three including travel.

Jennifer was not the least bothered and there was no point in complaining.

Swift was turning straight round to leave the building when she was intercepted by the woman she regarded as the Chief Constable's spy.

"Do you want this book on Icelandic culture?" Jennifer asked Swift.

The detective sergeant looked at her blankly.

"Why on earth would I?" she asked incredulously.

"I don't know," Jennifer said. "It's just that Paul asked me to keep a lookout for one in the secondhand bookshops on Steep Hill and this is the best I could come up with."

Swift hated the familiar way that Jennifer, a mere administrative assistant, referred to Detective Inspector Amos and she hated even more the fact that he didn't seem to mind. Nonetheless, she took the book from Jennifer's outstretched hand.

The cover was adorned with various representations associated with Iceland, such as geysers, fishing boats and snow scenes superimposed on a map of the island. Something caught her eye.

"It'll give me something jolly to read on the train, whenever I manage to catch one," Swift said sarcastically.

Jennifer merely smiled sweetly and sat down behind her desk.

As Swift feared, it was well into the afternoon before she reported for duty in London. The good news was that DS Gerry Burnside was in Norfolk helping with that end of the operation. The bad news was that it was Wednesday evening before Swift was back in Lincoln.

No one at Lincolnshire HQ was expecting her to return until the following afternoon: it was her own choice to suffer rush hour London Underground trains to St Pancras to catch a crowded service to the East Midlands.

Swift rang Detective Constable Susan Smith at home as soon as she reached her own house.

"I've been looking through Oscar Dover's accounts as you suggested," Smith said. "They're a real mess.

"It's quite evident that he kept them just to keep track of what he had bought and sold and where he'd stored them. If the Inland Revenue had ever caught up with him they would have had the devil of a job making sense of it."

"Do the accounts mention Grainger at all?" Swift asked.

"No," Smith replied emphatically. "Not a single mention. I looked very carefully. Sorry."

"Are there any instances that stand out of Dover conning people into accepting peanuts for their stuff and then selling it on for a small fortune?" Swift asked without much hope.

Smith laughed.

"Most of the stuff he bought, there's no record of him selling," she said. "No wonder the shop and storeroom were so jam packed. But yes, just occasionally he struck gold. And would you believe it, the two guys we talked to called Charlie fit the bill."

Swift took a deep breath. Satisfied with the reaction, Smith continued eagerly.

"Charlie Jones, the first one we spoke to, sold Dover a pile of stuff all in one go. A few items are marked as having been resold. One in particular, a grandfather clock, went for fifty times what Dover had paid for the whole collection. It went to a saleroom in Lincoln, one that's taken quite a bit of stuff from Dover. In fact, it seems to have been his main outlet for selling stuff on."

"Probably far enough away from the people who sold him the stuff not to find out what it was really worth," Swift commented. "And Charlie Smethurst?"

"He seems to have fed stuff to Dover in bits and pieces over a period of several months," Smith replied.

"Are you sure?"

"Yes, I know he said he only dealt with him once but that wasn't true. One thing that Dover noted meticulously was dates. He seems to have used his logbook as a kind of diary as well. There's no doubt Smethurst was duped right royally. He's the one person who sold good stuff quite cheaply to Oscar Dover time and time again."

"Well done, Susan," Swift said appreciatively.

"There's something else," Smith said quickly in case Swift was about to terminate the call, "although it may amount to nothing. Dover sold some chairs and a couple of tables to someone called Joe. No surname. I wouldn't have thought anything of it but he seems to have come back to the entry later and underscored under it so viciously it went through the paper."

"What makes you thing he did it later?"

"The entry was in black ballpoint ink, which is what he used mostly, but the underscoring was in blue. He seems to have become obsessed with this Joe. His name is scrawled on margins of subsequent pages, always heavily underscored.

"Also he met Charlie Smethurst – at least I assume it's him, there's just the surname recorded – the day he was taken ill."

"Thanks Susan," Swift said gratefully. "And well done. Just one more thing. Don't tell anyone I'm back in Lincoln or that I've spoken to you."

Swift turned in early that evening in order to wake refreshed the following morning.

It was already turning into a beautiful sunny day as she climbed into her car, wound down the windows and set off for Alford. She wanted to arrive midmorning, half way between breakfast and lunch when the café in the Market Square would be slack.

There were, in fact, a couple of tables occupied, both inside despite the beautiful weather, presumably because the outside tables were bathed in very hot direct sunshine.

Not surprisingly, Janet Templeton, the owner, greeted Swift with a distinct lack of enthusiasm.

"One or two more questions," Swift said cheerfully.

"Not here," Templeton cut her off hastily.

"Sally," she called to a middle aged woman wearing an apron in the kitchen, "can you just keep an eye on things. I'll only be a couple of minutes."

"I don't know," Sally grumbled.

Templeton glanced anxiously at the customers, who had broken off from their drinks to witness what was happening.

"Just a couple of minutes," she repeated.

"This won't take long, will it?" she said with a glance at Swift as she opened the door to the café.

The café owner walked purposefully to a relatively quiet spot in the middle of the Market Square.

"Right," she said. "Can we get on with this? It's beginning to feel like harassment."

"You mentioned in passing, the first time we spoke, that you had bought some chairs from Oscar Dover," Swift began. "That wasn't quite true."

"Yes it was," Templeton replied testily but slightly warily.

"I think not. Your fiancée bought them – and a couple of tables as well."

"How do you know what happened? You been to a séance? Did Ossie tell you through a ouija board?"

"No need," Swift said triumphantly. "Dover kept records of sales and purchases. He clearly recorded that Joe bought them."

Templeton looked deflated.

"Well, he actually went to collect them and handed over the money but I gave him the cash to pay for them. Is that illegal? In any case, Ossie didn't know Joe."

"Don't be so naïve," Swift snapped. "Dover came to your café. He was bound to recognise the stuff he had sold."

Templeton remained silent.

"Oscar Dover became obsessed with Joe. I think he was jealous, that he still held a torch for you after all these years. Did he threaten to show Joe the photograph he had of you."

"No," Templeton gasped. She looked genuinely shocked.

"Did you beg him not to do so?"

"No. The photograph was never discussed. He never mentioned it and neither did I. I wish I hadn't been so stupid as to tell you about buying the tables and chairs, then you would never have known."

"Yes I would," Swift said. "The evidence was in Dover's accounts."

"Joe never found out about the photo," Templeton insisted. "I would have known if he had. Anyway, if you've been through the accounts you know that he cheated Charlie Smethurst. I didn't want to land Charlie in it but I've remembered that he was threatening Ossie the day before Ossie was taken ill."

"How do you know it was the day before?" Swift asked. "I heard that his sister Stella didn't tell anything about him being taken ill."

"That old busybody Liz Wareham was round questioning me. She thought just because Ossie was a customer here I'd know all about it. She kept going on and on about it. I was trying to run a café. Which, by the way, is what I'm supposed to be doing now, so if you'll excuse me I'll get back to my job before I lose all my lunch customers."

Templeton was striding back across the square before Swift could say anything more – not that she could think of anything more to say anyway. She returned to her car and drove round to find Charlie Smethurst.

The man greeted her with about as much enthusiasm as Janet

Templeton had done. This time he was in the house rather than the garden and Swift heard him call "It's OK dear, I'll get it" before the door opened and his cheery look was transformed to dismay in an instant.

"I need to talk to you again, Mr Smethurst," Swift said quietly. "It seems you weren't entirely honest with me the first time."

Mrs Smethurst was bustling into the hall as the detective sergeant spoke, her look being one of surprise at the unexpected officer on her doorstep.

"It's all right, dear," her husband said. "I'll deal with this. You go back to getting lunch ready."

Mrs Smethurst withdrew reluctantly and Mr Smethurst ushered Swift into the lounge, sat down and looked at the detective impassively.

"You didn't have just one sale to Oscar Dover before you rumbled him, did you?" Swift asked. "You felt he'd cheated you several times, didn't you?"

"I don't know where you got that idea from," Smethurst said evasively.

"From his accounts," Swift said simply. "He kept a full record of his buys and sells, complete with dates. He did very well out of you, didn't he?"

"Look," Smethurst said in a low voice, leaning forward in a conspiratorial fashion. "I was stupid. He could be a very charming and persuasive man when he wanted to be. That's why I was so angry when I realised what sort of man he really was and said I wouldn't sell him anything more. I couldn't let Jessie know how stupid I'd been. That's why I had to make out it was just the one time."

"That's not the only thing, is it, Mr Smethurst?" Swift persisted. "You said that after Oscar Dover threatened you with the heavies you went to find him but didn't. But you did find him, didn't you? You found him sitting out at the café in the Market Square where you knew he always sat, come rain come shine."

Smethurst shifted uneasily and glanced round to see if his wife was opening the lounge door. Mercifully, there was neither sound nor sight of her.

"I suppose Janet Templeton has ratted on me," Smethurst said. "I don't suppose she told you we were queueing up to have a go at him that day. Her precious Joe was next after me."

"Never mind about other people," Swift said. "I take it you are not denying that you went straight to Dover and had it out with him? You knew where to find him."

"Actually, I didn't know where to find him," Smethurst retorted. "He wasn't there, and he wasn't at his shop. I went down the road to his sister's house but she didn't know where he was either. I'd just about given up when, on the way back home, I spotted him at the café.

"I begged him to back off but he wouldn't have it. Finally I resigned myself to having to let him have the stuff. But like I told you last time, he never came for it and no one else came so I thought he must have let us off the hook after all."

"Except he conveniently died," Swift said caustically.

"Look, what's this all about?" Smethurst suddenly demanded. "Am I accused of something? I didn't actually assault him – not like Janet Templeton's boyfriend did. Since she's obviously landed me in it, let's see how she likes it."

"I'm looking into Oscar Dover's business practices," Swift was able to say almost truthfully. At least now she could cite a genuine reason for her questioning. "Some of his associates are in police custody helping us with our inquiries."

Smethurst seemed mollified.

At this point Jessie Smethurst entered the room carrying a tray of sandwiches and tea.

"Oh dear," she said to Swift. "I'm sorry but I didn't think of bringing you anything. Charlie has diabetes and we have to eat at regular intervals. He needs his meal now or his sugar levels will drop."

"Don't worry, I'm just leaving," Swift said.

It might be useful to keep Charlie Smethurst onside by not embarrassing him in front of his wife.

Chapter 25

Ten minutes later DS Swift was parking her car in the Market Square. She suddenly felt hungry after seeing someone else's food and was mentally debating whether to risk going to the café and ordering a meal when she spotted Janet Templeton's fiancé Joe sitting alone at an outside table.

He soon became the third person in quick succession to greet her arrival without enthusiasm. The sun had now clouded over and the wind seemed chilly, leaving Janet Templeton's finance cupping his hands round his beaker of tea.

Having realised in her interview with Smethurst that she had a genuine excuse for making inquiries, one that would ring true, she immediately informed Joe that she was looking into Oscar Dover's business dealings as part of an inquiry into a group of people who had been arrested.

Joe brightened immediately.

"That rules me out," he said. "I never had any business dealings with the toerag."

"You were on his books as having dealings with him," Swift said.

The man looked genuinely puzzled.

"Some tables and chairs," Swift prompted.

"Oh that. I just collected them for Janet. They were for the café."

"He seemed rather taken by you. Scrawled your name all over his ledger, he did, Mr …. I don't think I know your surname and Dover didn't use it. Just Joe. Over and over again. Why do you think he did that?"

"I've no idea and I'm afraid you won't be able to ask him now so we'll never know. And the name's Johnson, for what it's worth," came the bland reply.

"I think Dover was jealous of your relationship with Janet," Swift said.

"I don't think so. Why should he?"

143

"Because he carried a torch for her. Didn't you know?"

Johnson fell silent. Clearly he did know.

"I think he had kept it all under control," Swift continued. "He was content to sit at her café, seeing her and speaking to her every day, and that was fine as long as he felt closer to her than anyone else. Then you came on the scene and were taking her away from him. I don't think he realised how close you and Janet were until you turned up at the shop and collected the stuff for her.

"That's when he snapped."

"Did he?"

"So he showed you the photograph. The one he had of Janet. And you saw red."

Johnson quietly put down his mug and turned to look at Swift.

"What's this got to do with Oscar Dover's business dealings?" he asked coldly.

Swift improvised.

"When a man at the centre of a police inquiry is threatened, as you threatened Oscar Dover, it becomes a matter of interest."

Suddenly Swift spotted a parking warden moving between the parked cars in the middle of the square.

Normally she wouldn't have bothered about collecting a parking ticket as she could easily get it revoked but this time she didn't want to run an unnecessary risk of anyone finding out she had been in Alford rather than London.

Without a word she raced across to forestall the telltale slip of paper. It took only a few moments but when she turned round to return to the café, Johnson had vanished.

There seemed no point in pursuing him. She did not know whether he had taken the left or right fork out of the top of the market place and even if she got his address from Janet Templeton he was unlikely to have headed home.

Instead, she decided to confront Oscar Dover's two daughters one last time.

Julia and Lynn were both at home, eating lunch in the kitchen. Swift could hear a short, sharp argument between them over who should answer the door, before the younger daughter finally did the honours.

Lynn reluctantly allowed the detective sergeant entry into the house. As soon as Julia saw who the visitor was, she exploded.

"What did you let her in for, you stupid girl," she stormed at Lynn. "Hasn't she caused enough trouble? I knew I should have answered the door myself."

"Why didn't you, then?" Lynn replied petulantly. "No one was stopping you."

"I'll deal with this," Julia said, leading the way into the lounge. "You go back and finish your lunch."

Julia did not offer Swift a seat. Indeed, she herself remained standing.

"What is it this time?" she demanded.

Time was running out. Swift was always more inclined towards the direct approach rather than Amos's softly methods. Now surely was the time to grasp the nettle.

"You stole the chemical from the school, didn't you?" she said abruptly.

"What of it?"

"Look me straight in the eye," Swift demanded, "and tell me the truth. I'll know if you're lying. What did you do with the chemical you took from the science lab at school?"

Julia Dover stared hard back at her.

"I gave it back to Tim," she said slowly and coldly. "Tim Armstrong."

Chapter 26

At this point DS Swift ran out of luck in catching people readily available. She drove to the school where Tim Armstrong was the chemistry teacher only to be informed by the headmaster's secretary that "Mr Armstrong rang in sick today".

"Did he say if it was anything serious?" Swift asked anxiously.

"I don't think so," the secretary replied without any signs of sympathy. "He said he would be in tomorrow. I certainly hope so. We can manage today but it's GCSE chemistry tomorrow so we need him."

If it wasn't serious, then there was no harm in calling at his house. However, Armstrong did not respond to a ring on the doorbell, although Swift could clearly hear it ringing in the interior. Armstrong would have had to be a heavy sleeper not to be awakened.

Swift looked up at the front windows. All the curtains were open. So, too were the ones at the back, as she discovered when she made her way round the building. There was no sign of Armstrong visible through the downstairs window, but there was a bowl with a spoon handle sticking out, a beaker, a milk carton and a cereal packet on the table. Armstrong had apparently been well enough to eat but not to clear his breakfast things away.

A small suitcase, unzipped but empty, lay on the floor with a few random items of outerwear scattered round it.

As Swift retreated to her car, the next door neighbour greeted her.

"He'll be at school, love," the neighbour remarked cheerfully. "He was a bit later than usual this morning but I saw him driving off."

Somewhat concerned, Swift hastily made her way back to Lincolnshire Police Headquarters, arriving in mid afternoon as if she had just returned by train from London. Nor did it look in any way amiss when she put out an alert to all ports and airports to watch for Tim Armstrong, as this could well have been connected to the Vice Squad inquiry.

"Ah, good, you're back," Jennifer said as soon as Swift put the phone down. "I was afraid you'd get tied up in London and I would have to redo the rota."

Swift tried without success not to look puzzled.

"Don't forget you're on duty on Saturday."

Swift had indeed forgotten.

It got worse. She soon found herself roped into an investigation that occupied the rest of the afternoon and most of Friday. She barely had time to put in a call to Armstrong's school. He was still off sick.

By Saturday teatime she needed a day's break.

By Monday morning, as she and Amos arrived within seconds of each other, there had been no further progress on the Oscar Dover front.

Nor had there been any reports of Tim Armstrong trying to leave the country.

"I'm now quite certain that Oscar Dover was murdered," Swift told Amos immediately. "And I know who did it. The problem is proving it."

She explained all the relevant details of the case that she had uncovered since Amos had been seconded to the education project.

"I see your point," the inspector replied after a few moments thought. "It all adds up. Let's tackle your suspect together and see what happens."

"It's Portsmouth Docks," Jennifer suddenly butted in. She was holding the telephone. "They've got Tim Armstrong. Shall I put the call through to your desk?"

"Put it through to my office," Amos ordered.

"You can take the call there," he added to Swift. "This is still your case."

Swift bustled into Amos's office with unseemly haste and grabbed the receiver.

"Putting you through now," Jennifer said with her customary

sweetness.

Swift was reassured to hear the click as Jennifer put down her own phone. She didn't want the conversation to be overheard.

"It's Frank Roberts, Port of Portsmouth Police. You put out an alert for a Mr Tim Armstrong, schoolteacher, white male aged about 35, dark hair, five feet eleven, medium build. We've detained him about to board a ferry to Cherbourg.

"He's travelling with a female aged 18, name of Dover."

"Wow," Swift said. "I hadn't reckoned on that. It's Julia Dover, I take it. She's actually 21 and left school ages ago so there's nothing to stop them travelling together."

"No," the voice at the other end of the line answered. "Lynn Dover. She says that as she's finished her A-levels she's left school so we can't arrest him just because he was her teacher and in a position of trust. Now she's left school she says she can do as she likes."

Swift paused for thought. They must have been forming a relationship while she was still a pupil so technically she could have Armstrong arrested for abusing a position of trust. However, if she was travelling with him willingly, what was the point?

"What do you want us to do with them?" the voice cut in.

"Let them go," Swift said. "Let them go."

Then to Amos, she said: "I think that settles it. That's why Julia lied that she'd given the chemical back to Armstrong. She picked on him out of spite because he had transferred his affections to her sister.

"Now there's no doubt who killed Oswald Dover."

"We'd better go through what you're going to say to her before you confront her," Amos said. "At least we can do it here in the privacy of my office."

"She's pretty hard bitten," Swift replied. "In my view only an outright accusation is likely to shift her. Maybe somewhere, just somewhere, she's kept a piece of evidence. The urn with traces of his ashes, say. If we get a confession I can apply for a search warrant. That might cause her to crack completely."

"It'll be worth a try after all the effort you've put in," Amos agreed. "The drawback of the perfect murder, the one you get away with, is that you can't have the pleasure of boasting about it without giving the game away. The temptation to tell the world how clever you've been can be overwhelming."

"We have to face the real possibility that she won't break, though," Swift admitted.

"In that case," Amos said in a sorrowful tone, "you'll have to let it go. There is absolutely no chance of getting a conviction without a written confession. Pushing the matter will achieve nothing except to destroy your enhanced status at HQ."

As at the start of the case, Amos and Swift made the journey eastwards from police HQ to Alford, this time in silence.

As they once more followed the winding road down into the town, Amos said: "No one could have achieved more than you did, Juliet," he said. "Thanks to you a paedophile ring has been broken up. And if it's any consolation, Oscar Dover was punished for his part in it."

"Let's not go in with a negative attitude," Swift replied. "Let's see if we can crack it."

Stella Dover met them on her doorstep with her customary "hmmph".

"So he's turned up again, has he?" she said to Swift, nodding at Amos as she did.

"Never mind the pleasantries," Swift said, pushing past her into the house.

"I suppose you'd better come in as well," Dover said casually to Amos.

Once inside, Swift wasted no time in launching into the speech she and Amos had rehearsed before they left HQ.

Chapter 27

"Stella Dover," she said. "You killed your brother, didn't you? When you blurted out to your friend Mrs Wareham that you didn't know who had murdered him, that was a lie, wasn't it? You knew perfectly well who had killed him because you had done it yourself."

Dover remained silent, for once not even emitting a "hmmph".

"I'm not sure what pushed you over the edge to kill your own brother. You had lost control of him and he had given the family home to his daughters.

"But I think what really got to you was when a parcel of photographs was delivered here by mistake instead of to his junk shop and you suddenly realised the depravity he had sunk into.

"You started to kill him bit by bit, using the chemical that Julia had stolen from school and which you had confiscated from her. No one would be suspicious if he died after a long illness. Then when Charlie Smethurst told you that your brother had threatened him and his wife you realised something had to be done quickly.

"I was told a parcel was delivered to the Dragon's Den by mistake and there were ructions. I thought that must refer to Oscar's friend Joseph Grainger and his den of iniquity. It didn't. You were the dragon.

"Dragon's Den was a little joke, prompted by your curious house name Lyngbakr's Lair. I don't suppose the postman understood who Lyngbakr was, and neither did I. I thought the map on the plaque at your front door was the Isle of Wight.

"It was Inspector Amos who recognised it as Iceland. According to the book of Icelandic myths, Lyngbakr was a sea monster that lay silently in the ocean looking like an island to lure fishermen to their doom. Poor Oscar never suspected that you were as much of a monster, in your way, as he was.

"Julia wouldn't admit to taking the chemical because that would have pointed the finger at her own aunt. No doubt she couldn't believe that you would kill her father. Even to the end, she tried to steer the blame away from you by claiming she'd returned the stolen chemical to the school.

"You were the one who had loads of opportunities to poison him and he would never suspect you. You made sure he was cremated against his express wishes. You scattered his ashes so we couldn't analyse them. You got rid of his computer discs. You burnt the pornographic photographs.

"In other words, you set out to destroy every shred of evidence."

"Yes, I did receive a packet of photographs," Stella Dover said. "One of them was of Lynn. His own daughter. How could he?

"When I confronted him it all came pouring out about the dirty old men who sent pictures to each other. Even then I didn't know he'd actually abused Lynn as well as making her pose for a nude photograph. She didn't tell me about it until after you first came snooping round.

"I could hardly believe it. I'd never suspected anything. She told me that was why Oscar had given them the house. It was to buy Lynn and Julia's silence. That was why I decided to let them keep it and make peace with them.

"Julia's a bright girl. She realised what I'd done with the stuff I'd taken from her. But she also realised that something had had to be done about the monster that her father had turned into."

Dover stared at Swift for a few moments. It was as if Amos was not in the room.

Then she spat out: "Prove it. Oh yes, you've been very clever. But apart from allowing myself to be provoked by that interfering busybody Elizabeth Wareham, I've been more clever. I was always one step ahead of you.

"And just in case you've got a tape recorder running in your pocket, I'm admitting to nothing. The truth stays between us."

Stella Dover was right. They would never prove anything. What she had said did not amount to a confession that could be used in court and she would obviously not sign one willingly. The only consolation was knowing that Swift had been right all along. Oswald Dover had indeed been murdered.

Swift and Amos looked at each other. They had agreed that at this point they would give up and Swift was about to do so when Amos spoke first.

"Stella Dover," he said, "I'm arresting you on suspicion of the murder of your brother Oscar Dover and attempting to pervert the course of justice. Give her the caution, Juliet."

A surprised DC Swift read a grimly silent Stella Dover her rights.

Dover was sure that Amos was bluffing. He had to be. She determined to call that bluff. Though she was now rather more circumspect.

Nonetheless, some of the bravado returned as the three of them left the house and walked to the police car. Elizabeth Wareham, the woman who had instigated the investigation, was walking down the road.

Stella Dover waved cheerily and ostentatiously to her before almost jumping into the car. Wareham received another cheery wave out of the window as the car swept past her. Then Dover sank back into sullen silence for the rest of the journey to Nettleham.

Amos steered her straight into an interview room without offering her the option of contacting a solicitor. As it happened, she didn't need one. She had had her gloat at her home and her moment of glory in front of Elizabeth Wareham. She really had nothing more to say. Since Amos had not bothered to switch on the tape recorder, it didn't greatly matter much anyway.

Finally, Swift asked if she could have a private word with Amos and the one-sided interview was suspended.

The corridor was empty.

"Look Sir," she said urgently, "We're never going to get enough evidence for a conviction. Or any evidence at all for that matter. I'm not downhearted.

"No one could have achieved more than I did. A paedophile ring has been broken up and at least there's the consolation of knowing that Oscar Dover was punished for his part in it."

"There's one last thing we can try before we admit defeat," Amos said. "We can hold Stella Dover for a few hours. We'll leave her to kick her heels in a cell."

Minutes later, Amos and Swift made yet another, final, dash across the Lincolnshire Wolds, this time to Louth. Julia Dover was at home.

"I thought you said you weren't reporting me to the Job Centre," she mistakenly fired off at Swift as soon as she opened the door. "Now I've lost my job and my benefits."

"In that case," Amos replied smoothly, "You have time to come with us to Lincoln to assist us with our inquiries. Your aunt is already there."

"If she's landed me in it," Julia exploded with her customary stream of expletives, "she'll soon wish she hadn't. I want to talk to her. I want to know what she's said."

"All in good time, all in good time," Amos said genially. "Let's get you to Lincoln and we'll take it from there."

All three maintained a stony silence until they were at HQ.

Amos and Swift got out of the car first. Amos spoke quickly across the top of the car before a reluctant Julia emerged.

"Put her in interview room 2," he told Swift. "You sit with her but don't say anything."

Once the two women were seated in the interview room, Amos went off leaving the door ajar to find a burly police constable who could stand by the open door for five minutes with strict instructions to restrain Julia if she tried to leave.

Then he went to find Stella Dover languishing in a police cell.

As Amos had hoped. Interview room 1 was also available. To reach it from the cells, it was necessary to pass by the open door of room 2 in full view of Julia, who leapt to her feet and made in vain for the door in an attempt to intercept her aunt.

For the first time, Stella Dover was rattled. Amos ushered her quickly into the vacant interview room 1.

"What have you brought her in for?" she demanded.

"Supplying the murder weapon, helping to dispose of evidence," Amos replied simply. "How about that for a start?"

Dover went into a deep thought.

"Julia did no such thing," she finally said emphatically.

"We'll see what she has to say for herself, then," Amos replied.

Another long silence ensued before Dover spoke again.

"I'll make you a deal," she said.

Amos noticed that the woman not said "Hmmph" once since her arrest. She had been knocked out of her stride.

Thus emboldened, he said: "I don't do deals."

"You'll do this one," Dover said. "My confession and a guilty plea and you let Julia go. She's too young to have a criminal record."

The remark carried the implication that Julia had indeed committed a crime, and that could only be supplying the chemical knowing what her aunt planned to do with it. However, the chances of nailing both of them were zero. Stella Dover was the bigger prize.

"This conversation hasn't taken place," Amos said. "But if you take full responsibility we would have nothing to charge Julia with. It's up to you."

"Hmmph," Stella Dover finally said.

An hour later, with a full confession written and signed, Amos returned to a thoroughly bored Swift and Julia Dover.

"Thank you, Miss Dover," he said smoothly. "We don't need you any longer. You're free to go."

Then to Swift he added: "Everything is all wrapped up."

Amos escorted the young woman to the exit to police headquarters.

On the doorstep, he told her: "If you walk down to the A158 you can catch the No. 6 bus to Horncastle and change there for the bus to Louth. I'm told it's a bit of a pain these days but I have been assured that it can be done."

ALSO BY RODNEY HOBSON

Detective Inspector Paul Amos Series

Book 1: Dead Money
Book 2: Unlikely Graves
Book 3: Holy Murder
Book 4: Kith and Kill
Book 5: The Hanging Tree

Printed in Great Britain
by Amazon